NIGHT TERRORS

VOLUME 1

Written by Peter Cronsberry, Tarphy W. Horn, K. M. McKenzie, Emil Pellim, Ryan Benson, Rosie O'Carroll, C. B. Channell, A. M. Todd, Karl Melton, J. M. White, Bob Johnston, Warren Benedetto, and Ron Ripley
Edited by Scare Street

ISBN: 9798680227008

This is a work of fiction. Any resemblance to actual persons, living or dead, or actual events is purely coincidental.

Thank You and Bonus Novel!

Thank you for your ongoing support. Our commitment to publishing bone-chilling horror would not be possible without you.

We appreciate you and would love to send a FREE full-length horror ebook, guaranteed to send chills down your spine!

Download your full-length horror novel, get free short stories, and receive future discounts by visiting www.ScareStreet.com

See you in the shadows,
Team Scare Street

TABLE OF CONTENTS

Cool Air

By Peter Cronsberry

Evelyn Holmes worked the crevice in her forehead the way a kid picked away at a scab. This wrinkle was so deep, a mother spider could have laid eggs in it. Or so she thought.

"I may *be* seventy-five, but I'm not going to *look* seventy-five," she rasped out at her reflection in her bathroom's medicine-cabinet mirror.

With gnarled fingers, she gripped the basin as tight as her late husband, George, gripped the steering wheel before he crashed their car and killed himself. Heart attack. Dead before his car hit the bridge abutment. Those business trips all over the country she thought he was on? Casino slot machines had never lost their appetites.

The downtown life and that three-thousand-square-foot condo in swish Lincoln Park was in Evelyn's rearview mirror. She's been a midtown gal for a few years, now. She'd shared a second-floor rental apartment with a mouse that played hide-and-seek, where paint had curled in hard-to-reach places, where the mechanical groans of her fridge signaled it had reached its best-before date, and where central air had been nothing but a pipedream—cruel punishment on a July day, where a breeze felt like a blast from a hairdryer.

She held dear her photos, memories, the illusions of yesteryear's marriage, and some newly-made friends who knew more about the treasures found in thrift stores than the contents that once filled her Gucci handbag. Strange as it seemed, she accepted her circumstances, part of which would change when she heard the eventual snap of the mousetrap.

Evelyn was always a people person. Her bird's-eye view of the street directly below was home to a dry-cleaner's, a fabric shop, and a health food store that cozied up to a gym where she admired the svelte and the chiseled as they came and went through its front entrance.

Her pension check covered the rent. There was enough money to put food on her table, buy the yarn for her knitting and the crossword-puzzle books she hoped would keep her mind sharp.

But way back when she turned fifty, thoughts of trying to keep Death's bony hand off her shoulder always filled her head. Now, when she went to the druggist's for her prescription, she bought what her budget allowed in the way of lotions, potions, ointments, and herbal remedies as she tried to keep her appearance. Too bad that gravity and the calendar had other plans.

To Evelyn, getting old had as much appeal as curdled milk. And as George's car barreled at a hundred clicks toward that bridge with one hand clutching his chest, she had her hand on the telephone to call Dr. Wilcox, who she'd heard seemed to work miracles with injections, but indecision stopped her dead in her own tracks, so to speak.

She also believed in luck, and if there was a pocket in any of her garments, a penny was surely tucked inside. Why, there wasn't a table, nightstand, bookstand, or countertop in her apartment that wasn't topped with an acorn or dice or even a wee figurine of an elephant she'd saved from a box of Red Rose tea. All were feel-good objects that helped her cope in the down-market life that defined her days on this rock.

So, there she was, dressed in a white, floral sundress, big sunglasses that shielded her baby blues and her pumps that cushioned her tender tootsies as she strolled along a sidewalk of an old part of downtown where dollar stores, burger joints, and supposed antique stores studded the streetscape.

She called it luck that she happened upon one of those supposed antique stores. She sidestepped a fallen bird's nest and cast her eyes up above a mud-colored wooden door and read the paint-chipped wooden sign: *Uncle Odds Emporium of Curios and Antiques.* Then she looked at the front window of the place, and when she saw a mannequin of a faceless magician, a mottled, slab tombstone, and even a model crypt with a pair of hands that grabbed on to barred doors—*from the inside*—she knew she had found something special. Intrigue grabbed her by the throat, and she pushed against the door that screamed against warped wooden floorboards.

Once inside, she was greeted with a scratchy-sounding, "hullo" from the back of the place. She walked over to the front of a broken-tiled aisle and discovered what was behind the disembodied voice.

He was an old man dressed in a rumpled white shirt and appeared as if he was being swallowed up in the seat of a black leather chair's cracked and bleeding white foam rubber. And as this genial gent pushed himself up and though hunched, he shuffled his way up the aisle with his arms bent at forty-five-degree angles at his sides that gave him the look of a sheriff in search of his gun. He had black, button eyes, a mouthful of stained and broken teeth, and a shock of thick white hair that stood on end and made him look like he'd peered into the bowels of Hell. Squatted atop piles of dusty tomes were statues of a Minotaur, serpents and beasts with long, yellowed teeth. These creatures seemed to guard not only the passageway but their caretaker as well.

When he moved past her, he stood beside a Victorian fireplace dusted with black soot and busts of King, Lovecraft, Grant, and Cushing that sat sentinel on its mantel.

She stole one more glance back at his perch and noticed that beside an old gilt-colored cash register stood a bookcase that was fashioned out of a lidless, upright coffin.

"You've got a bird's nest down on the sidewalk in front of your store," she said with a dose of sympathy. "Bad luck, you know."

"For me, or for the bird?" he said with a wry smile.

Evelyn blushed.

"Yes, I know," he started, as he wiped his beak on a hankie with dime-size tombstones printed on it. "I was just about to go out and sweep it up. It got knocked down last night from that little tremor the city had. 'Bout two in the morning it was. You feel it?" Then he shoved the hankie into his crypt-grey khakis.

"Well, a storm woke me up. I just thought it was one of those foundation-shaking rumbles of thunder. I'm in an apartment building. No damage, though. The news this morning said that there were lots of cracked windows and a few house alarms that went off."

"This town is never quiet," he said, almost as if he knew more than she did.

"Well, there was enough of a commotion to upset the world of a poor sparrow."

"She'll rebuild. Have a look around. There's something for everyone. Are you looking for anything in particular?"

"Yes. I'm looking for, well, don't laugh, but I'm looking for something that might bring *me* some luck," she said. She seemed almost spellbound by the Gothic charm of sepia-toned plaster walls pimpled with sconces straight out of a crumbling castle. She arched an eyebrow at the sight of a stuffed raven, its claws curled around a branch fastened to the wall opposite the fireplace.

Then she looked down at a table that showcased some of the most macabre objects she'd ever seen: three rusted embalmer's tools tied together with barbed wire, a meat grinder with bits of *something* in its cogs, and a thick, dusty, leather-bound book that said THE DEAD in old spidery script. Bound obituaries, maybe?

But when he saw her put her hands on the grey blades of an old fan, he suspected an imminent sale. "Ah. A perfect choice," he said as he hobbled over to her. "'Specially in this kind of heat. Heat like this can kill a person. That little gem is in perfect working order. Brought it all the way from Europe."

"Europe, you say?" she said, more fascinated than unsettled by his wares.

"Yep. Every few months I go over there on a buying trip. As you can see, I carry some of the more, shall we say, out-of-the-ordinary items. Nothin' wrong with a conversation piece, is there?"

"Or for nightmares," she said and offered a genuine smile. "No offense," she finished.

"None taken. Thanks for the compliment," he said.

She looked back to the fan. "Nothing unusual about this. It's just a fan."

"Oh, that's not just any old fan. No, it's one-of-a-kind. Silent. Light as a feather. Come on over here and I'll plug it in."

He picked up the little beast and she followed him over to an electrical outlet set into the wall just below a watchful grey gargoyle. He plugged the fan in, and without a squeak, creak, or groan from age, its blades began to whirl.

"Listen," he said.

"I don't hear anything."

"Exactly! No sound to bother you when you're watching television or trying to sleep. Do you have a window to put it in? Gotta be a south-facing window, 'cause it'll not only cool you down, it'll bring you luck."

"Well, I'm not sure what direction my living room window faces, but it's big enough for this fan. It'll look just darling in it. I'll take it!"

"Wonderful! Just one more thing."

"Yes?"

"This fan here, it has special properties. Are you close to a place where young people go? You know, an arcade or a gym, that kind of thing?"

"Why, yes. There's an athletic center that's right across the street from me."

"Now, isn't that fine? You just put it in the window that looks out onto the gym. The cool air its blades generate combined with all that healthy energy wafting over from the gym will take years off your life. No disrespect, ma'am, but you'll *feel* younger and you'll *look* younger."

"I can't say no to looking younger, can I, mister—"

"Odds. Just like the sign says."

"Well, I'm going to put it in my window as soon as I get home. Thank you so much!"

"You're very welcome. I'm glad you stopped by."

"So am I, Mr. Odds. So am I."

She watched him wrap it up for her the way Santa would an elf with a gift at his workshop.

About a half hour later, she walked into her apartment, went straight to her living room window, and got a welcome-home blast of hot city air in her face.

"Goodbye, heat. Hello, refreshment. And maybe even a new me," she said, positively giddy.

She took her prize out of her cloth shopping bag, held it in front of her and then positioned the fan in the window's sill. Then she turned it, so that it faced inward and plugged it into the outlet down below.

"Oh," she said to herself as she looked out onto the street. "I think I'm facing west. Doesn't matter. A fan's a fan." She shrugged her shoulders and then smiled when she caught sight of a virile man who carried a workout bag into the gym.

Satisfied, Evelyn stood there with her hands on her hips and a smile stitched on to her face as she watched the blades whirl in silence. Cool waves of air started to soothe the slack skin on her arms, legs, and especially her face.

She poured herself a glass of lemonade and then sat in her chair in front of the fan. She closed her eyes and felt its breeze as it played with the ends of her white locks.

She shifted her hand that brushed against the long-handled mirror she always had tucked in beside the seat cushion. Every day, she gave her face the once-over, always on the lookout for fresh wrinkles.

And every day, she took her supplements she bought at the health food store. She dabbed on her facial creams after she showered in the morning and every night before she went to bed.

Three weeks went by since she'd adopted her mechanical child, and one day when she was hosting a game of Bridge, Hilda Barrows told her how much more relaxed she looked. Penny Watkins thought Evelyn's complexion had changed and her best friend, Dottie—brazen as she was—said Evelyn needed to fess up as to her miracle cure: her wrinkles were *disappearing*.

Evelyn could have purred like a cat over their compliments. And with each one, she looked over to the fan and then caressed her face and said that she'd been trying a new face cream she'd discovered at an out-of-the-way merchant's, but its location stayed mum! She wasn't haughty, holier-than-thou, or conceited, but she sure as hell wasn't going to tell them what she *believed* was working the *real* miracle.

The next morning, she opened the *Chronicle* to the crossword to make sure that her brain was still firing on all cylinders. But there was one part of the paper she never did read, and that was the obits, because reading them would make her feel like she was crawling into her own coffin.

By mid-morning, she went out and ran some errands, and the praise kept right on coming. The checker that bagged her groceries, the clerk that signed out her library books and the residents she ran into in her building—they all commented on how *different* she looked. But it was Jalinda Williams who put the icing on Evelyn's cake when she said to her, "Girl, you look like the good Lord gave you back ten years on your life. Wait! Make that fifteen!"

July winked at August, and that ushered in waves of heat that made the city folk feel like wet dishrags. But the heat never seemed to bother the twenty- and thirty-somethings she saw at the gym's entrance. They looked energized when they went in and pumped and smiling as they wiped their foreheads with their towels when they came out.

Shadows from city buildings loomed like hungry monsters over her apartment building as Evelyn sat in her chair and knitted. She put a hand to her face, felt how smooth her skin had become, and then she craned her neck to give her fan a coveting glance. She reveled at what Odds had said to her about the connection between the fan and fitness, and as she pulled her mirror out from behind the cushion, she looked at her reflection and said, "Just how young could I look?"

She knew how important exercise was, and every day after lunch, she went for a walk around the block of her building but always on the east side of the main drag. She wore her dark sunglasses, her pumps, and the sun visor that looked like a bird's beak, and off she went.

And on her little sojourn, she passed outdoor patios where she heard people who gabbed and griped about the city or their neighbors. And one of the things she heard so often was their complaint about how little green space there was. Didn't matter whether it was downtown or midtown, people wanted to feel the coolness of natural shade, hear and see some birds, and look at earthy green instead of ash grey.

Around four o'clock, Dottie popped over for a chinwag and to watch their soap opera, "Days of Our Lives," and once that was over, they played a quick game of cards. Dottie felt the heat close around her like an unwanted embrace. She coaxed stray strands of grey hair back into her bun, and she noticed how often Evelyn looked over to the fan. "You expecting a gale out of that thing to *really* cool this place down?" she asked.

"Hmm?" Evelyn said. "Well, it's been working wonders for me ever since I bought it."

"You never did say where you got it from, anyhow? Fess up. I ain't never seen one like that at Canadian Tire or Walmart."

"That's because I didn't get it at Canadian Tire or Walmart."

Dottie put her cards face down and said, "Okay. Then where did you get it?"

Evelyn pursed her lips then looked at her cards and said, "I found it at a place downtown called Uncle Odds something or other."

"*Uncle Odds!* Oh, Ev, surely you didn't go in there!"

"And why not?" Evelyn asked.

"It's a morbid shop run by an old fool. If you ask me, the only day that that store should be open is Halloween!"

"I'll have you know he sold me that fan at a real good price. Said it came all the way from Europe."

"Hah! Rubbish! It won't last the summer! You watch!"

"Have you ever gone into Odds' shop?"

"Nope. Wouldn't be caught dead in there. Saw him once in his front window, and he looked like he crawled out of his own grave. I've heard whispers of bad things that happened to some folks that bought some of his junk... deadly junk that belonged more in a ghoul's garage sale."

"Name one!"

"I heard tell of a man who bought an urn there, and then he started killin' people. And then there was a guy who bought a painting from him, and a ghost came out of it. The ghost haunted him so bad, the man died of a heart attack right there at his wife's graveside. If I were you, I'd get rid of that thing before it—"

"Before it what? Kills me, too, Dottie? Listen, that fan's done me a lot of good. Besides, he told me I should put it in a window facing a gym because it would take years off—"

"Oh, now I get it. Lemme guess. He told you you're going to look years younger if you just let the young vibes and the cool air waft all over you."

"That's not fair!"

"'Tis fair. Just looking out for you, kid."

"You told me yourself that you thought I looked younger."

"And you do! Everybody's noticed. But really, Ev, a little old fan, mystically can do what a tube of cream from a drugstore can't?"

"I believe him, Dottie!"

"The devil's snake-oil salesman is what he is. You believe what you want, but I still say that that old warlock sold you a bill of goods. Your play."

"Look at my face, Dottie."

"Your play!"

"Go on. Just look at my face. You see any wrinkles? Every one of those cracks has practically gone away ever since I got that fan and put it right there in that window."

"Across from the gym, no less. Ev, honey, do you hear what you're saying? It's all a lot of hocus-pocus."

"It isn't hocus-pocus! It isn't! Dottie, my bones don't crack near as much when I walk, and I feel like I've got more energy."

"Listen, if you think it's working for you, then that's all that matters. You tell the other girls?"

"Of course not. They don't need to know, and please don't say anything."

"Are you kiddin'? They'd have the men in white coats over here pronto. Okay, Ev. Have it your way. My lips are sealed. Let's get back to the game. Your play. But I'll say one last thing."

Evelyn hung her head as she waited for the next salvo.

"If you do turn into this fifty-something siren and you see some eligible men come out of that place, wouldja steer 'em my way?"

All of a sudden, laugh lines appeared on both their faces. They finished their game and parted with a hug.

But Dottie's hit-job on Evelyn's rejuvenator wasn't going to change a thing. Evelyn babied it. She cleaned it. She smiled at it. She pleaded with it to never give up the ghost. And her silent partner just kept right on giving, as it turned left to right, left to right...

But as we all know in life, a little rain must fall. The next day, she was startled out of her nap by the sound of shouting down at street level.

She got up out of her chair, looked out the window, and noticed a cluster of workmen dressed in dusty jeans, bright orange safety shirts and hardhats—all of them standing on the gym's front steps. They looked like bees in front of a hive. She couldn't quite make out what all the fuss was about, but the more she looked, the more she noticed there weren't any people dressed in workout clothes that went into or came out of the place.

The workmen moved to the far right-hand corner of the gym. Two men looked at what could have been the building's blueprints while a third man put a tape measure against the wall, and the fourth walked to the opposite end of the building. She figured they were going to fix the front steps, maybe sand down the concrete or whatever they did to repair cracks. *Buildings aged just like people did*, she thought to herself. So, she didn't think anything more about it and went back to her fan therapy and dozed off again.

But the commotion across the way was as unsettled as was the city.

She was awakened shortly after to the sound of hammering. She got up out of her chair, looked out the window, and noticed workers were putting up hoarding in front of the gym.

Like a cat, curiosity got the better of her. She had to find out what was going on. She put on her pumps and headed on over to the gym. She marched up to the hoarding and was met by a big beefy man, somewhere deep in his forties, dressed in a navy shirt, jeans, white hardhat, and he carried a clipboard. He was writing something, but she couldn't see the pen that seemed to be all but swallowed up in a thick puffy hand. When he saw her, he stopped writing, put his arms up, and told her to keep back.

It turns out that there was more to that earthquake a few weeks back than what she or even Odds knew. Mr. Construction told her that the rumbling that that tremor caused, managed to shift the building's foundation. There were thick dark cracks that looked as if a giant spider was going to push its way through the cinderblocks in the building's basement.

But the worst of the news was what he said to her next.

"So, your men are here to fix it?" she asked, full of presumption.

"Fix it? Oh, no, ma'am. This building, she's being prepped."

"Prepped? What does that mean?"

"For demolition, ma'am. It's too unstable. The foundation has been so badly compromised from the inside that we've got orders and rightly so, to tear 'er down. Place could pancake at any time."

Her eyes were so wide you'd have thought she'd dreamt of seeing herself at her own funeral.

"But they'll rebuild, won't they? Put a new gym in this one's place?"

"That's up to the city, ma'am. And politicians being politicians, well, they're bound to do what they set their minds to, and sometimes us regular folks don't have a say in the matter. I'm really sorry, ma'am, but I'm going to have to ask you to keep clear of this sidewalk. S'too dangerous. You never know, an aftershock could hit and take this building down in a heartbeat."

"Yes. Yes, of course. We don't want anybody getting hurt," she said.

"I've got to get back to my men. No disrespect, ma'am, but if you could cross at the lights and use the sidewalk on the other side of the street, please."

She was speechless. Deflated and with her head down, she looked like she'd just been handed her eviction notice. She shuffled to the traffic lights and then trudged across the street to her apartment building.

When she came through the building's lobby, she ran into the Super, Scotty McTavish. She quizzed him about the goings-on at the crippled gym, and he no more knew what was to replace it than the date of his nephew's birthday. But he was sure whatever took its place, it'd be commerce because the city was too hard up for cash, so a new gym seemed to make sense.

Once she got inside her apartment, she got on the phone to Dottie and apprised her of the situation. "They'll rebuild. They just have to!" she said. Dottie tried to calm Evelyn's nerves by agreeing with her.

She spent so much time in her chair she felt she needed to be close to that fan now more than ever.

She couldn't get interested in any of her TV programs. The tea in her cup went cold, and a fly found the untouched biscuit on her plate. She started to knit, but then she stopped, and all that grey yarn made it look like she had a mess of intestines in her lap. She wasn't even half-interested in knowing whether Randall was going to propose to Charlene in her romance novel. She just plain looked like someone up and told her Christmas was cancelled.

But her constant companion remained so, as its head kept on rotating left to right but with the horrible news delivered: its cool air felt grave cold.

Evelyn never was one much for sleeping late, and these days, she was up before five just as the birds were greeting the city with their warbling cheer. But on this particular morning, it wasn't the robins that roused her from her slumber.

It wasn't fingernails on a chalkboard, but it was pretty damned close.

It was the sound of metal that scraped on pavement and diesel exhaust that belched from the smokestack of an excavator's cab. From due north, it crawled its way toward the construction site, and once it arrived at its target, a team of workmen descended on the thing like worms to a carcass.

The red ball of fire had just poked its nose over an eastern skyscraper, and the time was a whisker shy of 7:00 AM.

Evelyn pulled a supposed lucky penny out of her shorts pocket and clutched it like it was a panic button. And there was her little helper perched in the window with its head that turned left to right as if to say "No!"

She looked like a human gingerbread lady with her arms bent at her sides. She gulped in some air and slow-walked it to the window, terrified to look.

It was cause enough for a heart attack.

Wrecking machine. Two great big steel pincers at the end of a long boom positioned at two o'clock, and in short order, a man seated inside its cab would move levers that would send those pincers goring into the concrete sarcophagus. Even the burly boys in their dump trucks were lined up at the corner ready to haul away the rubble to a roadway being built along the eastern shore.

She heard the beast of a machine hiss as it came to a stop and watched as a few men gathered around to talk the mission over.

Hard to say whether it was fate or coincidental planning as she and Dottie were headed to a mall to do some shopping and then stopped off at a botanical garden to peruse the posies and walk the hedgerows—a small antidote for avoiding the impending dust and destruction. By about half past seven, she'd left her apartment without so much as a nod to her faithful friend.

Twelve hours later, the dust hadn't quite settled, long after the yellow behemoth collapsed the structure in on itself.

Evelyn walked into her apartment looking like a mourner headed graveside with Dottie acting as a pallbearer. Dottie huffed as she took off her shoes while Evelyn padded over to look at the mole of steel and glass that had been cleaved off a slab of concrete skin. She turned the fan on, looked out, and when she turned back around to Dottie with such a horrified look on her face, she clapped a hand over her mouth. All she could do was point backward toward the window and the carnage across the street.

Dottie asked, "How bad?"

Evelyn went and stood in the kitchen, closed her eyes and shook her head.

Dottie marched over and looked out to the gray gash in the streetscape. She turned around and said in no uncertain terms, "You know what this means, don'tcha?"

"My death. But I'm sure you'll find a way to put a positive spin on all this."

"You're damned right. And quit with the dyin' talk, will ya? That hole across the way ain't gonna stay a hole forever. You know why? 'Cause I'll just betcha the city's got a mind to put a newer and better gym right where the old one stood. You just watch!"

Evelyn put a hand to her face and felt a wrinkle coming on as her eyes rimmed with tears.

"And stop bellyaching about your looks. You want to think that a piece of junk from a kook's shop is gonna help keep ya young, you go right ahead, but your real answer is—"

"That fan! And that gym!" Evelyn shouted.

"No, they ain't!" Dottie shouted back then dialed down her tone.

"Then how do you explain the wrinkles on my face that disappeared, Dottie. Now they're coming back!"

"Creams! You said it yourself, you found a special one in some *secret* place. Well, maybe it ain't so special! Find a new one. Or two. Ev, honey, no matter how much we all wanna turn back the clock, the truth is we just can't."

"You think I'm being ridiculous."

"You're not ridiculous. I'd never judge you. You've got friends that love you for who you are and wrinkles be damned. Ev, we're of an age where hucksters have old folks like us in their crosshairs."

"Dottie, I don't want to get old!"

"You think I do?"

"But—"

"No buts! You saw how quick they tore out that gym. They'll rebuild. You'll see. Have some hope. Keep the faith, kid."

"I *still* think there's something to that fan. And when that gym gets rebuilt, I'll look—"

"I'm not going to tell you to throw that fan away. I'd be happy to do it for ya, but if you really think— Listen. Get some rest. Don't forget, you, me and the girls are going to see that George Clooney picture tomorrow. Now, *that's* the kind of rejuvenator we all need!"

"The popcorn's my treat."

"That's my girl. Chin up. I'll see you in the morning."

Their parting hug had a way of casting a ray of sunshine on a very stormy day.

At a little before midnight, Evelyn lay awake in her bed with her hands at her neck as she felt for loose skin. Then she heard a rumble of thunder, birthed from a storm cloud that stalked from the west at sixty clicks. She turned her head toward the window, and the last thing she saw was a claw of chain lightning that forked in the distance. Oddly enough, the rain lulled her into such a deep sleep she never did hear the crash of two mature trees just behind where the gym once stood.

The next morning, she padded into the living room and turned on the fan without so much as a glance at the remains across the street.

Then she went into the kitchen to see to her breakfast, and the teacup she pulled down from the cupboard slipped from her fingers and *ker-smashed* on the parquet flooring.

That brought a couple of choice curse words from her lips.

When she finally managed to set a cup of tea to steeping, her hand knocked the sugar bowl and sent a white spray across the counter.

"Goddammit all to hell!" she shouted. "Well, Lord, I'm all yours! Things come in threes, so bring it on!"

A couple of minutes later with her cuppa finally fixed, she was ensconced in her chair with the fan blowing cool air through her locks.

She turned the television on, and straight away she put a hand to her forehead and felt for wrinkles.

But she could only stew for so long. Her sideways glances were a little shy on results, so being a beggar for punishment, she got up out of her chair and looked over at the section of street that looked like a row of teeth with one missing from the inside of a boxer's mouth. But this time she noticed something different on the site's hoarding. There was a big white sign with what looked like lots of black lettering on it. Of course, she couldn't make out the words, but as sure as Monday followed Sunday, she got the idea into her head that it looked like one of those development signs that sprout up on vacant lots. Her jaw opened wide enough, a fly could have flown in and down to her stomach.

Right away she reached over to her table, grabbed her phone, and punched in familiar numbers.

"Dottie!" Evelyn shouted after Dottie picked up on the first ring.

"I'm here! What's wrong?"

"There's a sign on the hoarding at the site," she crowed and fanned her face so fast you'd have thought she had a mouthful of cayenne pepper.

"You got a pair of binoculars?"

"Nope. It's got to be a development sign, right?"

"Mmmm. Could be."

"Come on, Dottie! Now's the time for a hefty dose of that never-ending optimism of yours," Evelyn barked. "Get over here and let's go take a look. It's Saturday, so there aren't workmen there to shoo us away."

"I'll be there with bells on!" Dottie said.

Minutes later, those two old birds stood at the intersection waiting for the light to change when Dottie said, "Lotta damage from last night's storm. Must've been some wind. There's tree branches everywhere."

"Storm didn't cool things down much, did it? Oh, hell!"

"What is it?"

"I forgot my glasses," Evelyn said.

"I brought mine. C'mon, the light's changed. Let's see what the sign says."

The twosome beetled a diagonal line to the hoarding like they were about to charge the doors at a bingo hall. Dottie's agility got her to the gate first, and Evelyn brought up the rear as she puffed like a steam engine.

"Your get-up-and-go out of gas, girl?"

"Just a twinge in my legs," she wheezed out with her hands on her hips. "Enough of the sarcasm. Just tell me what the sign says."

Dottie put on her glasses and craned her neck as she tried to read all those black capital letters. She managed to read a few words then turned to Evelyn with a partial verdict. "Yep. It's a development, all right. Good sign, Ev."

"Does it say when they'll start to rebuild the gym? When will it be ready?"

Dottie read on and mouthed the words in silence. Then all of a sudden, her arms went slack and the expression on her face made it look like somebody had told her she wasn't going to get another Old Age Security check. She turned toward Evelyn, slowly.

"Well? Don't keep me in suspense. Tell me! What's the good news?"

"The development, Ev. They're going to build a little parkette," she said quietly.

"A parkette is good. Behind the new gym, right?"

"There's more, Ev. It's what they're going to *expand* from back there. And you'll likely be able to see it from your window."

"You're not smiling, Dottie. Expand? Expand *what*? What will I see? Spit it out! You're killing me!"

"The development, Ev. Ev, they're expanding the cemetery!"

Evelyn's face took on the pallor of a corpse on a mortuary slab. Her jaw hinged open. And as she turned and looked up, all she saw in that dark maw of her window was the head of her fan moving left to right... left to right...

* * *

THE PRESENTATION

BY TARPHY W. HORN

Sidney Wallace, through no fault of his own, arrived at the office late for the second time in five days. He told his boss, Wilshire, about the gruesome accident on the Interstate that stalled his commute for forty-five minutes.

"I don't want to hear your excuses!" the furious man shouted. "I don't care if Einstein came back from the dead, stood in the middle of the freeway, and handed out IQ points! If your sorry excuse for an ass is late one more time, you're fired!"

After stalking back to his desk, Sidney dropped heavily into his uncomfortable chair. A long, demanding day loomed ahead of him. The blood-red numbers on his digital clock already showed 8:47 AM He had only six hours until he made his presentation to the Board of Directors.

Unwittingly, he flashed back to the twisted mess of metal and blood splattered across I-35. He' d narrowly avoided adding to the five-car pileup. When the tiny Corvette ahead of him slammed on the brakes, he' d swerved out of the way. The driver of the black Ferrari he cut off blared on the horn and blew past him. The tiny Corvette slid under a flatbed trailer.

Sidney sighed. He needed to put the horrible experience out of his mind for now. If he couldn' t dazzle the Board and prove his worth to the Company, Wilshire would likely fire him. He' d already warned Sidney several times about his "low and substandard productivity and lack of motivation."

Wilshire was a jerk.

Sidney pulled the flash drive containing his presentation out of his pocket and plugged it into the computer. As he reached for the keyboard so he could log on, his large, overly clumsy hand knocked over a nearby Styrofoam cup. The remains of yesterday's coffee flowed across the desk, soaking papers, pens, his mouse, his keys, and the only printed draft of his presentation. The cold, brown liquid finally rushed into his lap and soaked the crotch of his pants.

Yelping in surprise, he banged his knee on the side of his desk. The cup couldn't possibly have held the volume of coffee that poured out of it. Frantically, he shoved his papers out of the way, but it was too late. He dried off his desk, then threw the ruined pages and soggy tissues toward the garbage. The already-overflowing can's precarious tower of slimy banana peels, half-empty cans of soda, wadded-up piles of paper, and other detritus toppled to the carpet.

"You've got to be kidding me. I can't do this right now!" he hissed. He reached down to pick up the trash and stuff it back into the can. As he leaned down, the seam at the back of his pants gave way with a loud RRRRIIIPPPPPP.

Great, now what? He couldn't deliver his presentation to the Directors with a giant hole in the rear of his pants.

Don't panic, he told himself. He opened the top drawer of his desk and reached inside. Maybe he could find something to fix the torn fabric. As he rummaged through his supplies, his fingers plunged into a large, sticky wad of gum. What in the world was gum doing there? He never chewed gum. Gross.

He wiped the offensive glob against the edge of his desk with a shudder. With a sudden, frantic spark of inspiration, he grabbed his stapler, bent over at the waist, reached around himself, and awkwardly stapled the torn fabric of his pants back together. It was a pathetic but effective solution.

Now, finally, he could stop wasting time and get to work. He needed to go over his presentation, so he didn't look like a blithering idiot in front of the Directors. Thanks to the coffee debacle, he had to print out another copy.

He typed in his password: 1GudGolfer. An error message beeped loudly on the screen, announcing that his password was invalid. He entered it again, slowly. A loud, angry, computerized voice angrily shouted that it was still invalid.

How can a computer sound angry? Sidney wondered. I must be imagining things.

Witnessing that accident must've stressed him out more than he realized.

Grinding his teeth, he dialed the Information Technology department. A sweet, automated female voice thanked him for his patience. She informed him that all technicians were busy, but if he would please leave his name, extension, department, supervisor's name, supervisor's extension, zodiac sign, and a brief description of the problem, someone would get back to him as soon as possible.

Fuming, Sidney said, "This is Sid Wallace. My extension is 437. My password isn't working. It's giving me an invalid password error message. Call me ASAP. This is urgent."

The automated voice instructed him to begin recording his message at the tone.

Biting his lip hard enough to draw blood, he repeated the message and hung up. Looking at his computer screen, he growled, "I should win an award for my patience."

The phone rang instantly. Scowling, he answered.

"Wallace."

"Hey, Waldorf. This is Ted from I.T. I understand you're having some trouble figuring out how to use your password," he said in a bored, condescending voice. "Have you tried retyping your password?"

Was this idiot kidding? Sidney bit down on his tongue to keep from calling Ted bad names. He needed his help, even if his tolerance level for grief from the I.T. department was at an all-time low.

A warm trickle of blood on his tongue and a rapidly swelling lip did nothing to improve his mood.

"Yes. I've retyped it."

"Type it again."

Marveling again at his own patience, he typed his password. "I tried. Again. That isn't the problem."

Ted droned on, with complete seriousness, "Is your computer turned on?"

"Of course my computer's turned on! How else would I know my password doesn't work?" Beads of sweat began forming on Sidney's face.

"Is the screen turned on?"

"Are you even listening to me?" Sidney asked tightly.

"Of course, Waldinger. We're here to help. Try retyping your password."

Sidney slammed the phone down in frustration. He planned to find the I.T. department later and pay "Ted" a little visit. He'd knock the teeth from his snide little mouth. First, though, he needed to get access to his computer.

As a last, desperate resort, he typed his password again. His home screen finally popped up. However, instead of showing the usual picture of three bikini-wearing beauties on a beach, the background now featured an erupting volcano.

Very funny, Ted. We'll talk later.

Shaking his head in exasperation, he clicked on the program to bring up the presentation.

Amazing, he thought. *The way this day's going, I'm surprised the file is even here.*

A message appeared on the screen: File opening... 10%... 15%... 25%... 26%... Sidney pulled the handkerchief out of his pocket and wiped off his forehead. His foot started tapping. The metallic taste of blood lingered in his mouth.

While he waited for his file to open, he leaned around the cubicle's partition to ask his coworker if her computer was acting up. The petite redhead was wearing a headset and clicking through data on a spreadsheet. Although she was wearing wool pants and a heavy jacket, she reached down and turned up her space heater.

Are you kidding me?

"Psst. Melissa?" he whispered loudly.

She turned to him, eyes bugging out, and gestured at her phone.

"I know! I know you're on a call. Could you just turn your heater down a bit?"

She rolled her eyes and shook her head, then returned her attention to her computer.

Fine, he thought. He pressed the switch to turn his desk fan on full blast. Nothing happened. Looking under his desk, he saw the cord laying on the ground. Groaning, he leaned down and plugged the fan back in. Behind himself, he heard RRRIIIPPPPPPP.

Sidney swore viciously. The hole in the back of his pants had doubled in size. He'd need to get more staples from the office supply room.

The screen showed his file was 33% loaded.

He squeezed his eyes shut and counted to ten. Taking a deep breath, he pressed the switch on his oscillating fan. Once again, nothing happened. Looking at the ground, he saw the cord was not plugged into the wall.

He must've snagged it with his foot and pulled it loose. With a grunt, he jammed the plug back into the outlet and turned the fan on. Blessed, sweet air blew immediately onto his sweaty face.

Sighing, he noticed the computer screen. File opening... 98%. Maybe this day could be salvaged after all.

The screen went dark.

Judging by the sudden outbreak of swearing in Spanish, English, and Hindi in the nearby cubicles, Sidney concluded a circuit breaker must have blown. He picked up the phone, squeezing the receiver in a failed attempt to control his frustration. A guy named Chuck answered his call to the building's maintenance department.

"Good morning, Chuck," Sidney said tightly. "It looks like we've blown a breaker here on the 26th floor. I'm on the north side of the building."

"You're outta luck, pal. The guy who flips the breakers is out sick today," said Chuck in a heavy Brooklyn accent.

Sidney closed his eyes before replying. "So, have someone else do it," he said between clenched teeth.

"Sorry, pal. Union rules. Can't do another man's job." Chuck hung up the phone.

Dropping the phone on his desk, Sidney slid back in his chair. He wiped some more sweat from his forehead, then got up to go to the electrical room. He'd flip the breaker himself.

The guy who flips the breakers, he thought incredulously. Does that lazy prick expect me to believe there's only one guy here who flips the breakers?

It took around fifteen minutes to find the electrical control room, locate the breaker panel, and reset the switch that had tripped. When he got back to his desk, he realized he'd forgotten to stop at the supply room for staples.

Whatever. One of his drawers held a roll of duct tape. He'd make it work.

Returning to his cubicle, Sidney turned his computer back on and reinitiated the slow process of opening his slide presentation. After securing the back of his pants with carefully placed strips of grey tape, he decided to get some water.

He walked quickly toward the break room, glancing at his diamond-studded watch. The face of the watch proclaimed 8:35.

"Great. The battery's dead," he muttered. His pants pulled at the awkwardly repaired and re-repaired seam, so he walked slowly with his legs close together.

He looked up just in time to see the very wide eyes of Alisha, the intern from the accounting department, as she collided with him. Folders and papers went flying, and her coffee doused the front of his shirt.

"Watch out!" he shrieked as he lost his footing and tackled her to the ground. Several nearby coworkers rushed to her aid.

"Watch where you're going, you giant oaf!" huffed one of the suits as he helped Alisha to her feet.

"Girl, you need to SUE his ass," said Melissa, the redhead from the cubicle next to his.

What?

"Misogynistic punk, thinkin' he can just walk wherever he wants to. Like you don't have a right to be here." A woman with brown skin and braids hanging to her lower back leaned over Sidney. "I got my eye on you, bitch."

Mutters and stifled laughter met his ears as he got up and hurried around the corner.

"Did you see the back of his pants?" a woman's voice drifted after him.

"Yeah. The cheapskate can't even buy new clothes when he needs 'em."

Every muscle in his body was tense as Sidney entered the break room and headed straight for the sink. He grabbed some paper towels and dabbed at his soiled shirt.

Sighing in defeat at the pointless endeavor, he picked up a Styrofoam cup and filled it with water from the water cooler. As he lifted the cup to his lips, the Styrofoam cracked from his overly intense grip, and cold water ran down his face to his shirt.

"I've had it!" he yelled to the empty break room. "I'm going home! I dare anyone to try stopping me!"

He threw the remains of the cup at the sink and marched out into the hallway. "To hell with all of you!" he growled at the small crowd standing around Alisha. He stomped across the office to the elevator while ignoring the looks of amusement from the people whose cubicles he passed. "To hell with all of you, too," he snapped, pointing a finger at each mocking face.

He stood at the elevator and jammed the down button with his thumb. He was wearing more coffee than he normally drank. Sweat poured off him like he was a perspiration fountain. Even his hair was soaked.

Turning around, he noticed every cubicle in sight had a space heater.

"It must be 85 degrees in here!" he whined in a high-pitched voice. "What the hell is wrong with you people?"

Every eye in the room stared back at him with mixed looks of amusement, irritation, or indignation. He shook his head. "For this, I'm still paying on student loans," he mumbled.

He stepped into the elevator when it finally arrived. The vomitous smell of flatulence, left by someone in need of immediate medical attention, assaulted his nostrils. He pushed "G" for the ground floor, then pinched his nostrils together. The doors slid shut. The elevator rushed down two floors, then jerked to a stop. The doors slid open to admit two overly perky teenagers. They wore pristine white tennis dresses and carried racquets. They stared at him judgmentally as they noticed the unfortunate odor.

"Rude," said one of them in a drawn-out, sing-song voice.

"It wasn't me," Sidney snapped.

"Sure, dude," said the other one, turning to whisper to her friend.

The doors slid shut. The elevator rushed down four floors, then stopped suddenly a second time. A man with a white service dog got in. The dog sniffed the air and whimpered.

The doors slid shut. The elevator rushed down three more floors, then stopped. Three women wearing business suits got in, and the teenagers got out. Sidney felt nauseated. He looked at the elevator's digital display. Seventeen floors to go.

Once again, the doors slid shut. Sidney tried convincing his stomach to settle. He shouldn't have eaten that third donut for breakfast, but he'd figured he wouldn't have time for lunch. The elevator seemed to pick up speed as it descended.

After ten floors, it stopped so suddenly one of the businesswomen lost her balance and fell against her colleagues. The women hastily left the elevator, and four pale, dark-haired men in black suits got in. The quartet stood in a row and stared at Sidney with vacant eyes. Sidney looked straight ahead at the doors and tried not to squirm. The uncomfortable situation didn't help his nausea.

When they finally reached the ground floor, Sidney took two steps out of the elevator and ran straight into Mr. Lentil, the building's superintendent. As he opened his mouth to apologize, his stomach succumbed to the day's stress. Sidney vomited on the man's freshly shined and obviously expensive shoes.

Lentil, who stood 6'4" and weighed about 230 pounds, looked down at the decorative remains of Sidney's last couple meals.

Last night's chocolate fudge strawberry supreme pie wouldn't be adding to his waistline, at least.

"You're coming with me, you degenerate thug," grunted Lentil as he grabbed Sidney's arm.

Sidney, feeling somewhat better after the sudden, violent purge, blurted the first words that came to mind. "Sorry! Wrong floor!"

The superintendent yanked him away from the elevator. "I don't care! You're coming to my office and cleaning off my—"

"Can't, my man. I'm late for a presentation!" Sidney twisted out of the giant's grip and fled back into the elevator.

"Hey!" yelled the indignant superintendent.

Sidney leaned against the farthest corner of the elevator and smirked as the doors closed. Getting away from his cubicle for a bit put everything in perspective, and he started to relax. Storming out of the building would've cost him his job. He'd give the presentation, and everything would be fine. He wasn't the first person to ruin their clothes before a big meeting. With any luck, he'd even have a chance to dim the lights.

A small, frail-looking, silver-haired woman with a cane stood in front of the number panel. She was going to the 40th floor. Sidney collected himself and asked politely, "Could you please press 26?"

She raised her crooked, wrinkled, middle finger, and didn't budge.

Feeling his last thread of self-control snap, he grabbed her and shoved her away from the control panel. With his attention fully focused on reaching the circular button, he failed to notice the woman's hand digging into her pocket. With astonishing speed, she pulled out a small, black aerosol bottle and sprayed him in the face.

Coughing, gagging, and screaming, Sidney fell to the floor.

"That'll teach you, ya fat creep," the old woman shouted in a crackled, long-time smoker' s voice.

Sputtering, he managed, "I'm just trying to get to my office!"

The elevator stopped on the second floor, and the doors slid open. For the first time since he was twelve years old, Sidney began to sob. The tears stung his already violated face. A young, professionally dressed couple looked from Sydney to the snarling old woman.

"We'll take the next one," they said in unison.

The elevator wobbled up to the third floor. A man with pale skin, a long black cape, and teeth filed down to sharp points came through the doors. Sidney wondered if the blood on the cracked corner of his mouth was from another person.

On the fourth floor, a woman with elegant makeup and a parrot on her shoulder strode in and stood to the right of Sidney.

"Jackass," the parrot said. Its beady black eye met Sydney's. "Jackass," it repeated.

Sidney's still-stinging face was undoubtedly red and blotchy. His right eye was beginning to swell shut. *Maybe that'll keep the Directors' attention off my torn pants*, he thought. *Ironic.*

A delivery man was waiting on the fifth floor. He wheeled in a cart that held a box roughly shaped like a coffin. Morbidly, Sidney wondered if it held the remains of the Corvette driver from this morning's accident. The delivery man turned the cart around and backed up to stand right in front of Sidney. Sidney yelped involuntarily as he stomped on his feet.

"Move it!" the delivery man griped.

"Jackass," said the parrot.

Sidney didn't bother responding. He was too tired.

The elevator stopped on every floor. Sidney realized that although people were getting in, no one was getting out. The air became stale, and Sidney wondered how many more people the elevator could hold. It had to be approaching the weight limit.

He'd been standing there for at least twenty-five minutes. At this rate, he'd miss his meeting with the Directors. Restless and panicky, he glanced at his watch.

8:35. Damn, he forgot the battery was dead.

"Anyone have the time?" he asked.

"Jackass," replied the parrot. No one else said anything. The parrot's owner wore earbuds and was utterly oblivious to her bird's vulgar comments.

On the tenth floor, two middle-aged women joined the group.

"I'm telling you," said the first one, "that boy is bad news. He'll have Sabrina knocked up in no time."

"Sabrina, ha!" answered the second woman. Sidney cringed at the shrill tone of her voice. "That little slut deserves what she gets. She's slept with half the boys in town and a few of the girls! I've even heard she's had abortions."

"Absolutely scandalous!"

The elevator lurched to a stop. Sidney's nausea returned with a vengeance, and the loud, judgmental gossip session didn't help. A girl with a large boa constrictor wrapped around her body squeezed in next to the pair of women, who looked at her disapprovingly.

"People who bring exotic pets into public spaces are rather rude, don't you think, Marla?" Bitty Number One said to her friend.

The girl turned to glare at the women, and the snake hissed. Sidney didn't think Snake Girl looked like someone to mess with. Marla sniffed. Vampire Guy checked out Snake Girl with obvious interest.

As that drama unfolded, the elevator stopped on the twelfth floor and picked up a big, burly, sweaty man with a toolbox. He smelled of acrid sweat and urine. Incredibly, no one else seemed bothered by the horrendous odor.

The tennis girls would've passed out, he thought.

Sidney decided to get out on the next floor and take a different elevator. He just had to figure out how to get past Delivery Guy. He shifted his weight to the left and tried to see around him. He would have to plow his way around a few people, but he didn't care. The elevator was definitely past its weight capacity.

Sidney waited while the elevator ascended. The sound of the groaning motor made him nervous, but at long last, they made progress toward the 26th floor. Sidney realized that also meant they were getting further from the ground. If the cables holding their car gave out, they'd have no chance of survival. He felt like he'd been buried alive.

After several more seconds, the elevator stopped. Sidney figured they'd reached at least the 20th floor. However, when the doors opened, the screen overhead flashed the number 14.

Maybe someone was playing a practical joke on him. Maybe he was on one of those reality shows where they pranked unsuspecting people. What if one of these weirdos was filming him, or there was a camera in the elevator?

He closed his eyes. I will not succumb to paranoia.

A man with a spiked mohawk and a wide, toothy grin strode into the elevator. He carried a butcher knife. His leather jacket had silver spikes sticking three inches off the shoulders. To Sidney's horror, but certainly not surprise, the man pushed his way to the back of the elevator and stood at Sidney's left side.

"Suck my cock," commanded the parrot.

The man leaned down until he was inches from Sidney's face.

"What'd you say to me?" He continued grinning like a maniac.

This is it, Sidney thought. *A stranger is going to murder me in an elevator because of a rude bird.*

"I didn't—it wasn't—" he stuttered.

"Suck my cock," the bird repeated. It hopped on Sidney's shoulder and relieved itself. Warm, greenish-yellow ooze slid down his shirt.

The man on his left continued to grin, with his horrible teeth and putrid breath.

Sidney shoved the bird off his shoulder.

"Jackass! Suck my cock!"

Maybe the elevator cables would break, and he could fall to his death and finally get some peace. This was like an express elevator to Hell. He wanted to scream, but he knew if he started, he wouldn't be able to stop.

They arrived on the 15th floor. People were already packed together like sardines, but somehow a young mother with a crying baby and a wailing three-year-old squeezed in with them.

"Mama!" the toddler screamed. "Mama! Mama! Mama! Mama!"

"Suck my cock," the parrot demanded. "Your mama sucks my cock!"

Marla, speaking loudly so her companion could hear her over the chaos, complained about a neighbor's dog who kept digging up her flower bed.

Grinning guy sneezed on Sidney and continued grinning.

On the 16th floor, an Elvis impersonator got in. The old woman with the pepper spray and bad attitude held the door open for him.

"Thank you," he said in a perfect imitation of Elvis. "Thank you very much."

Sidney couldn't take anymore. His sanity had been slowly deteriorating for about seven floors now. He roared, the adrenaline-fueled burst of anger exploding from his lungs in an almost visible cloud of energy. Startled passengers raised their eyebrows or giggled. Sidney shoved his way through the wall of bodies. The doors slammed shut just before he reached them.

They stopped on the 17th floor. The doors opened, revealing a brick wall. Hysterical laughter erupted from his mouth. Tears and snot erupted from other orifices, and the others on the elevator began shirking away from him. He clapped his hands.

"Good one, guys! Good one!"

By the time they reached the 20th floor, he'd pulled himself together. He used his handkerchief to clean off his face, taking great care to avoid his swollen eye and irritated skin. The elevator doors opened, and he flung himself into the lobby. He landed on his hands and knees in front of a group of men and women in military uniforms. They looked at him disdainfully, then walked around him and got in the elevator.

As the elevator doors closed, he heard the bird cheerfully shout out, "Jackass!"

He stood up, checked that his pants were still somewhat repaired, and looked at his surroundings. The immaculate hallways, leading in three different directions that formed a "T," looked the same as those on most of the other floors. Closed doors flanked the plain walls. The hum of a cluster of vending machines was the only sound. An acquaintance from the purchasing department strolled by and nodded at him. Sidney walked to the lone window and looked out at the dreary day.

Maybe the constant stress of the job was finally breaking him. He knew the human resources office hadn't moved from the 17th floor. He'd obviously hallucinated the brick wall. Maybe it was time to think about switching careers.

The stairwell was just to the left of the elevator. Climbing six floors would probably be the fastest and least stressful option. Sidney pushed against the metal bar on the door to gain access to the stairwell and began to climb up.

By the time he reached the 22nd floor, he was feeling the effects of his lack of regular exercise. His breath came in wheezy gasps, and colored spots danced through his field of vision. His heart fluttered like the wings of a panicked bird.

Gulping air as he passed the 24th floor, he leaned forward and half-crawled up the stairs. When he reached the 26th floor, he wondered if he could get to his desk before he passed out.

With his eyes watering and still half-shut, his rubbery legs made their way uneventfully through the office to his cubicle. He collapsed into his chair and slid immediately off the front of it. The chair rolled out from underneath him, dumping him on the floor with a graceless thud. The remaining staples in his pants dug into his skin, and he felt tiny spots of warm blood soak into his underwear.

His computer screen showed that his presentation file was 98% loaded. Swiping at his eyes, he looked at the time on his desk phone's LED display. It showed 9:15 AM.

That's simply not possible, he thought. I've been in this building for at least three hours. But the phone, his digital clock, and the computer system all agreed. He hadn't even been here an hour.

Looking again at his expensive watch, he noticed one of the diamonds was missing from its setting. He began to laugh and found himself unable to stop. Melissa, the girl across the aisle, told him to shut up so she could concentrate.

"Wallace! Keep it down over there!"

His supervisor appeared out of nowhere and hovered over him. Sidney began to offer a scathing reply when he noticed the title slide of his presentation appear on his computer screen. It read: "How to Increase Productivity and Avoid Wasting Time on the Clock."

The irony would have sent him into more gales of hysterical laughter, but he envisioned himself standing unprepared in front of all the suits in the boardroom and came back to his senses. His supervisor scoffed and moved on.

He scrolled through the slides, familiarizing himself with the information. "We could increase productivity by 135%, simply by stretching out the length of an hour," he said to no one in particular. This time he couldn't stop the fit of giggles until he heard his supervisor's footsteps heading back toward his cubicle. He quickly cleared his throat and continued looking through the file, until the shrill ringing of his telephone interrupted him.

"Wallace," he answered.

A deep voice shouted, "You're late! The Board is waiting! Get your ass down here or you're fired!" The line went dead.

"But that's impossible!" Sidney howled, looking at the time. It read 3:02. He should've had hours to prepare yet. Had he fallen asleep?

No. He hadn't. Standing up and looking around the office, he saw everyone diligently working at their computers or talking with coworkers. Why hadn't anyone else noticed weird things happening?

He didn't have the luxury of taking time to find out. Quickly, he resaved his presentation to his flash drive and raced to the boardroom. He pulled open the heavy wooden doors. Twelve sets of eyes stared at him coldly.

"I, uh, apologize for my appearance. It's been a trying day."

"You were late to work, and you were late to this meeting. What do you have to say for yourself?" demanded his boss. He put out a cigarette in the ashtray in front of him.

"I'm sorry. Let me get the file upload going, so as not to waste any more of your time," Sidney said nervously.

He dropped the flash drive on the plush red carpet, and they laughed. He felt an angry flush heat his face as he picked up the tiny device. He inserted it into the laptop on the table and opened his file. The title page of his presentation appeared on the giant screen at the head of the room. He cleared his throat.

"Today," he began, "I'd like to present to you the findings of my study on how to increase productivity."

He clicked to the first slide. Anger swelled in him as everyone in the room began to laugh again. Looking behind him, he saw that someone had tampered with his file. A gory photograph replaced the chart he'd painstakingly created.

"Hey! Who changed my file?" he yelped in a high-pitched, panicked voice. "What the hell is that?" He gestured forcefully at the photo displayed on the screen.

"Don't you recognize it? Look more closely," instructed a man sitting at the far end of the table. Sidney couldn't make him out in the dim light, and he didn't recognize his voice. He looked at the screen.

"Oh god!" Sidney said in astonishment. "That's the accident I saw this morning! That's the reason I was late!"

The Directors laughed harder. A few laughed so hard they gasped for breath. Finally, the man shrouded in darkness spoke.

"Wallace," the deep voice said, "that accident is not the reason you were late. That accident is the reason you are dead."

Sweat poured from Sidney and stung his widening eyes. Realization struck him like a thousand volts of electricity. Stumbling, he ran toward the door. As he reached for the door handle, it disappeared. A brick wall stood where the door had been. As he whimpered, he heard more shrieking laughter from the Board.

His boss composed himself enough to ask, "What's the matter, Wallace? Aren't you enjoying Hell?"

* * *

The Homeowner's Guide to Sanity

By K. M. McKenzie

The cozy little townhouse drained my budget, but the neighborhood was quiet. Traffic didn't exist.

My own place at last.

I, Lotte Norwood, was a homeowner.

These were the things I noticed during my first week: My neighbors were quiet people. Cars came in and cars went out. Few young children.

I would have to get used to working from home three days of the week. There wasn't much I couldn't get done from a computer these days. I put up sticky notes on my office desk: remember to call parents, contact the office, buy groceries, and so forth.

I met my neighbor during the second week, waving to him from my office window while he mowed his lawn.

"I'm Lotte," I said.

"Wilfred." He pointed to himself. "I thought someone moved in recently."

"Yeah, it's been a week."

He made a face. "You alone?"

I didn't feel comfortable answering that question as a woman. I considered lying but summoned a half-truth. "My brother comes and goes. You might see him stop by from time to time."

He nodded.

Wilfred knocked on my door some days later. "Sorry to bother you," he said softly. "My wife's wondering about the work you're doing on the house."

"Handyman stuff?" I thought he was seeking employment.

"I heard a noise last night. Are you fixing something? I don't mind, but it was quite loud."

"I'm not working on the house."

He frowned. "Are you sure? Because it was pretty loud."

Maybe he thought I was lying. "I'm pretty sure."

"It wasn't your brother."

"He's not here."

"Well then, never mind," he said.

That was strange, I thought as I marched back to my office room. The neighbor had a problem with me after only one week.

Wilfred returned the next day, more irate than before. "It's the sounds again. Drumming and nature music," he said. "I'm sure it's coming from your house."

"No one plays nature music—certainly not me."

Wilfred screwed up his face, ready to argue.

I was in a good place and didn't want an argument. "Can you show me where you think the sound came from?" Maybe something caused the sound, a radiator or pipe or something brushing against another thing. The townhouse wasn't new—that's why it had been so cheap.

Wilfred led me around the side of the house, through the narrow pathway that separated my house from his. We stopped at the heating unit. It hummed. It was loud in my ears, but he didn't seem fazed by it, so I assumed it was at normal levels. To be sure, I asked, "This isn't what you heard?"

He looked insulted.

I often relied on other people's judgment to determine normal levels of noise. A marble hitting a wooden floor was loud for me. Might as well be a cabinet tumbling down a staircase.

We marched to the back of the house. He inspected the pipes and even the small shed in the backyard. There was nothing that produced a sound that could be mistaken for drumming or nature music.

Wilfred insisted, "I'm sure it came from the house."

"Why don't I look into it," I said to keep the peace.

"Thank you," he said, almost dismissively.

This wasn't what I'd hoped for. I briefly considered if he was trying to pull one over on me to drive me out. Maybe he didn't want to live next door to a young black woman. Maybe I was being paranoid. I decided to give him the benefit of the doubt. But, if someone was hammering, it sure wasn't me.

After he left, I marched down to the basement to look around. Before moving in, I upgraded the ventilation. That had delayed my move by a month.

I switched on the light and glanced around the small area. Olga, the old owner, had left me a nice glass-topped table with black iron-backed chairs with floral designs. They remained the only furniture in the basement. My goal was to rent the place out, but I wanted at least the first month to myself.

The tiny bedroom had newly varnished wood flooring. The vinyl windows were bigger—a necessary fire exit if I wanted to rent, according to the inspector. The window looked out to the side, facing Wilfred's house. This would seem the obvious source of any sounds.

The more I considered his complaint, the more insulting it felt. He might have been hearing some *other* noise. There was no one here to hammer or drum.

Still, I was a homeowner and had to take responsibility. I turned switches on and off and tested the air vents.

I tugged off a ply of toilet paper and pressed it against the air vent in the small bedroom. It stuck. That meant it worked. Everything worked, including the pipes that led out to the laundry machines, and the ventilation that led to the backyard. Nothing made a noise that could be described as hammering or drumming.

Just the humdrum sounds of whirring and... I cocked my ears to the pipes right outside of the bathroom.

Whispers. After my diagnosis of a sensory disorder, I discovered that there were people who could see ultraviolet light and ranges within a single color. There wasn't a term for people who could hear distinct sounds within sounds. My doctor had simply said I had exceptional hearing and warned I would go deaf if I didn't leave the city.

The distinct whispers coming from the walls mingled with the whirring and gurgles of the heating cylinders and plumbing pipes of the house. The whispers seemed to form a rhythm. One, two, three, four, followed by quick half-beats of up to twelve. They repeated the same pattern.

I pulled back with a pinch of concern but assured myself that the odd sound might still be part of the acoustics of the house. Nothing unusual. Satisfied that I had completed my part as a homeowner, I turned in to get some rest.

Wilfred didn't come back the next day. Admittedly, I returned to work, so I might have missed him. I woke that very same night to the sound of shuffling dishes. I dashed downstairs to find no one, except for a procession of black ants marching toward a crease in the floor.

For a quick moment, I thought the kettle had moved from where I'd left it but chalked up my newfound paranoia to Wilfred's influence.

Two days later, I arrived home to find my irritated-looking neighbor waiting outside. I was barely out of the car before he spoke. "It has gotten louder. I can't take it any longer."

"I have no clue what you're talking about."

"It's gone from bad to worse. Last night, I heard drumming, and what sounded like critters. Rub, dub, dub, rubber dub," he mimicked, before resorting to critter-insect sounds.

The man might be insane. Did I just inherit a neighbor from hell? "I'm gonna be honest. What you're talking about has nothing to do with me."

"It's coming from *your* house," he shouted.

"There's no one in my house that drums, whispers, or makes chittering sounds. No one and nothing."

"I think you should get a professional to take a look," he suggested.

I glared him down. "My house is perfectly fine, Wilfred. Have a good evening."

"Those guys you had fixing the place a few weeks back, it's as if they're still down there working."

"That makes no sense. You're hearing things that don't exist."

I hated myself for saying that last part. Before I was diagnosed with hyperacusis, everyone dismissed me the same way—treated me as if I was going mad.

"I don't know 'bout that," he shrugged, "But we can't sleep over here. And, if this keeps up, we're gonna have to file a complaint with the city."

"You know what, go right ahead." I pushed past him into the house, leaving him to stare.

Wilfred's absurdity wasn't what kept me up that night. The *whispers* did. They started to seep through the walls. I could hear the intentional pattern. The long notes and then the half-beats, repeating. That noise was distinct from the sounds of the pipes and the ventilation system.

I flew out of bed at the pummeling of my front door. One very confusing second later, I heard Wilfred's voice as he stood outside knocking. The hell. It was after one in the morning. I should have ignored him but threw on my robe and rushed to open the door.

"What do you want?"

"We can't sleep."

"That's not my problem." I glimpsed his elusive wife standing on the front steps of his house in a lovely night robe, hands crossed at her chest.

"We have complained repeatedly about the sounds..."

"I don't hear anything," I countered. A lie, sure, but even if those whispers were legit, there was no way Wilfred could hear them. Our homes weren't even attached.

Wilfred's face took on a bewildered expression. "Well, you have to get your hearing checked."

"My hearing is fine, thank you," I fired back. "I am the only one here. I was sleeping when you woke me up. How insensitive." I slammed the door in his face and returned to bed. I fully expected him to knock again.

Surprisingly, he didn't.

Wilfred got under my skin. Days after that confrontation, I got an inspector to examine the pipes and ventilation system. I had them do it on a Sunday when Wilfred was on his front lawn doing yardwork.

The inspector stood on my front lawn and said, "Everything's working superbly. Nothing broken or unusual."

After the inspector left, I waved to Wilfred. "See, nothing here." *Maybe you should get your ears checked.*

In the days after, I attempted to salvage my peace of mind. I started working in the basement, doing little paint jobs. I was ready to rent it out for extra income.

I convinced myself that its sounds were normal. The inspector had insisted the whispers most likely came from hollow spaces in the foundation.

This seemed perfectly logical.

Days later, I arrived home to find a notice stuffed under my door, addressed to Miss Lotte Norwood. The bastard had gone through with filing a complaint with the homeowner's board. I rushed to file my own complaint of harassment against Mr. and Mrs. Wilfred and Katerina Cyrus, most certainly the neighbors from hell.

Determined to fight back, I began knocking on doors around the crescent. I had two questions.

"Have you been hearing any odd sounds at night, drumming, hammering, or critters?" Wilfred's complaint had used all three terms that led me to think this was a campaign of harassment rather than a legitimate issue.

Most people shook their heads.

So only Wilfred.

My second question. "Have you ever had any issues with Wilfred Cyrus or his wife?"

That got a boatload of responses. Supposedly, he was petty. There were complaints about him measuring people's fencing, declaring himself the neighborhood watchman, and lambasting the previous owner of my house with accusations of misdemeanors.

"Olga had a tenant he didn't like, a quiet guy Wilfred accused of being a druggie and psycho."

I hit the jackpot when I asked people for their support of my counter-complaint. One person did throw a wrench in my perfect case.

"Olga's tenant wasn't a drug dealer, just weird," said the neighbor with the house behind mine. "The guy was always wandering up and down the street at late hours, whistling to the sky, howling and making all sorts of strange gestures, like he was an animal whisperer or something."

"Did she evict him?" I asked.

"He was her son. She wouldn't throw him out. Chose to just sell."

My case against Wilfred was still strong, despite the old tenant issue. Whatever his issues were with the old owner's son, it was an obsession he hadn't gotten over.

The next day, while I was doing some long overdue gardening, Wilfred's wife pulled up to their house. I hadn't exchanged more than two words with her. Instead of heading into her house, she made a beeline toward me.

"It's Lotte, right?"

"Katerina?" I only knew her name because she was a co-complainant against me. What did she want? "Is my gardening bothering you, too?"

She frowned, looked down, and then laughed. She seemed mild-natured, and maybe too good for her husband.

"I'm truly sorry, you know."

"For ruining one of the biggest achievements in my life, getting my first home?"

"You need to understand that it has been a nightmare for us since Olga's son moved in."

"What does any of this have to do with me?"

"There was something wrong with that boy."

"Which has nothing to do with me." Was she for real? "I don't know what you and your husband are hearing, but it's clearly in *your* heads and not the house."

"He liked music," Katerina insisted, indifferently. "He used to play at all hours of the night. No mercy. If we complained, Olga would fling curses our way. She said playing kept him *sane*. He whispered all the time—claimed he couldn't speak. He just whistled and whispered and played music. Wilfred thought it was intentional, that he was anti-social, and doing it to drive us out."

"Again, I have never met these people."

"Did you check the house properly to make sure he didn't plant anything there?"

The thought had never occurred to me. "You should check *your* house. See if he planted anything there. Maybe that's why you're hearing sounds." I threw off my garden gloves and marched into the house.

The truth could be maddening. I wasn't planning on wasting another four hundred dollars to ensure that the old owner's crackpot son hadn't planted devices in the house that went off at odd hours of the night. It was silly.

But it was hard to dismiss the whispers.

There was another matter. The whispers woke me that night, louder than I recalled ever hearing them.

The same beats and pattern.

I cocked my ears, listening. The sound came from the walls. A moth drawn to a flame, I descended to the basement.

The sound was isolated to the small bedroom. I switched on the light to reveal nothing out of the ordinary. The windows were bolted shut. There wasn't a hiding space.

I even opened the small closet to make sure.

The closet was put in by the construction crew. Surely, if there had been something odd, they would've noticed it—the inspector, too.

My hands vibrated when I touched the wall next to the closet. The trembles and whirs of pipes only. But underneath their mundane echoes were the whispers.

Maybe I was going mad. I crouched down and tucked myself inside of the tiny closet that was poorly illuminated by the light of the room.

What did I expect to find?

A beeping device? Signs that my hellhound neighbors had been right? Once, during the renovations, I came by to see what the construction crew was doing. My input wasn't needed beyond my instruction to the crew. They just had to fix the room up—change the windows, build a proper wall between the bedroom and the kitchenette, and create a pathway to the laundry space.

I had seen no evidence of fault.

Crouched down with my hand running against the back of the closet, I found what had not been there before and pulled back, panicking.

My instinct was to call for backup or, at least, get a flashlight. Instead, I dialed my brother's number.

"Landry, you need to get over here now."

When he pressed me to explain, I yelled, "It's an emergency."

I waited, eyes fixed on the back of the closet. An opening. Nothing came from it except air and... whispers.

Was this an oversight by the renovation crew? A soft spot in the wall that gave way? Something about it was too deliberate. How could the construction crew have missed this?

My mind returned over and over to Wilfred. Then I considered what Katerina had suggested. Was there truly something planted in my house?

The whispers grew louder all of a sudden. Because even the distant sounds drummed in my ears, I couldn't say how far away or close the source was. But they came from this hovel.

The sound of critters was an otherworldly echo, growing in volume as if a horde of insects was headed my way.

I backed out of the room and bolted the bedroom door in time to hear the crash against it—a slam so hard the door rattled as if it might break apart.

I was on the lower steps and rushing to get upstairs when the drumming started, stalling me for a mindboggling moment. It came from the small bedroom.

Horrified, I ran up the stairs and bolted the door to the basement. I couldn't remain in the house, so I grabbed my coat and settled on the front porch.

My thoughts were on fire. I paced the lawn.

What the heck was that?

I kept glancing at Wilfred's house. The lights weren't on. Were they asleep? Could they hear the noise?

My brother showed up an hour later, freaking out. "It's late, you know," he whined. "Why don't you get a man for this nonsense?"

"Shut up!" I yelled, shaking.

He studied me. "You okay?"

"Something's wrong with this house." I glanced at Wilfred's house, hating that he was right. Still, I knew what I witnessed.

"What's going on?"

"Just drive me away from here."

"It's those clown neighbors, again?"

I shook my head and marched to his car. Reluctantly, he got in and pulled out of the driveway. He didn't say anything to me until we were on the main street.

"Okay, start talking. Did they do something to you?"

"Something's living in the basement."

"What? What d'ya mean 'something?'"

"That noise the neighbors complained about, I heard it."

"What noise?"

"Something's not right. I can't even explain that sound."

He studied me. "You need to visit the hospital?"

I shook my head. "I just need to think."

Landry tossed every possibility at me while he drove.

"Are you sure those neighbors aren't trying to drive you out?"

"I don't know," I admitted. What I had witnessed was unexplainable. But I had to find out what lived in that crawl space.

Days later, a new inspection crew arrived.

A clueless-looking Wilfred stared out from his yard as the crew approached. "Are you finally fixing the problem?" he asked.

I ignored him.

The basement bedroom was empty. The door to the closet was closed—I didn't recall closing it. Even the crawl space was gone, sealed back into the wall as if it had never existed.

"Break it open!"

"Hold up, hold up," my brother said, a worrying look on his face. "Lotte, you sure about this?"

"Landry, I am honest-to-hell sure. It's either this, or I'm selling this house. I am not staying here without finding out what's there."

My brother nodded, looking concerned.

The crew pummeled through the drywall to reveal wood and metal pipes.

Landry peered inside the dark hole. "That's storage space."

The lead crewman said, "Two of us can go in."

Landry grabbed my hand and pulled me back. "These guys are the pros." His eyes suggested he was keeping me safe, just in case this went all wrong.

The lead crewmember stayed behind while the two younger guys crawled under, flashlights and construction equipment on their belts.

"What do you think is there?" asked the lead crewman.

"I don't know." I folded my arms over my chest and paced. The crewman called out to his men after a few minutes.

They didn't respond.

He picked up his two-way radio and called out to them.

No response.

"They can't be that far," he said, concerned. "Ricky? Daryl?"

The transmission crackled. A choppy voice came through, barely audible above the static.

"Ricky? That you? What are you seeing?"

"There's a tunnel," came the broken reply. He repeated his words a few times before we understood.

The lead crewman watched me. "Why would a tunnel run under your house?"

I shrugged. A tunnel? Maybe I hadn't heard correctly.

"There's a hole of some sort, like a room," came the voice through the radio. It broke up into static.

The leader called out, "Come again?"

The voices broke up choppily. "... here."

A cacophony of cicada-like sounds broke out.

"What the...?" Landry cut himself off, grabbing my hand. Horrified, we listened as screams broke through the radio transmission, drowning under the insect chitter.

Then there was nothing. Well, not for my brother, or the lead crewman who stared dumbfounded at the device in his hand before screaming for his men to answer.

They weren't answering.

What they couldn't hear was the calculated and steady whistling. The patterned sounds.

"I'm calling the cops," said the crewman beside me.

Nearly half an hour later, the firefighters and police arrived. They swarmed my house. Talked over and above me—they wouldn't send any more men inside of the crawl space.

They started bulldozing part of my house—my dream home.

The neighbors became spectators.

Wilfred looked neither happy nor satisfied, just bewildered.

Half of my house was leveled. My brother looked horrified. My parents, too. The entire damn neighborhood whispered and stared.

It was surreal. An entire underground pathway led deep into Wilfred's house. The construction crew dismantled a portion of his house—to his rage and defiance.

No one knew how it got there or what it was for.

The real horror wasn't the loss of my first home. That stung, while I sobbed into my mother's arms. What lay deep down in the ground would remain forever imprinted onto my brain.

The construction crew and firefighters rappelled themselves down, while a news helicopter flew overhead.

A swarm of insects broke free from the hovel, forcing the spectators to run for cover. They couldn't hear the whispers, but I could hear them from deep down into the hovel, where they echoed desperately, rapidly, horrendously.

More emergency workers roped down.

The deep underground maze had a junkyard's worth of musical instruments, crates and crates of what turned out to be insects and bugs. Hordes and scores swarming around in large transparent containers.

"What is going on?" shouted one of my neighbors.

A clash of sounds rung out from deep down inside of the hovel. Shouts and fumbling, things knocked over and thrown about.

"Grab him."

"Shoot!"

Gunshots ripped and ricocheted.

Then it was all over.

The cops dragged a bleeding, half-naked man to the surface, tied and cuffed, dirtied from grime, hair pasted to his face.

"Oh my lord," Katerina gasped, turning away.

As the muttering spread among the neighbors, I learned who the half-starved looking person was—Olga's son, Daniil Ivanisevic.

In the days and weeks to follow, while I fought with the insurance company about recovering the cost of my home, the truth about Daniil's underground horrors came into full light.

The cops charged Daniil with murder for the deaths of the construction workers, among a litany of other charges. His lawyers pleaded insanity.

Daniil fancied himself some sort of insect whisperer. As his sanity declined, he began to whisper and whistle as a form of communication.

A failed musicology student, the mentally disturbed Daniil convinced himself he was working on a theory of insect communication, believing that insects could be controlled with music.

He had been training the swarms that he lured into the hovel, building contraptions. Most of his construction equipment sat on the side of the house closest to Wilfred's.

It seemed Daniil had plans to extend his insectarium even deeper under Wilfred's house.

At the very least, Wilfred and Katerina dropped their legal complaint against me, and I, in turn, did the same, turning my rage and desire for compensation toward the previous owner.

When contacted, Olga claimed that after she kicked him out of the house, she lost contact with him. I didn't believe a word that came out of her mouth. She did know that her son had been building an extensive underground hovel beneath the house to carry out his experiments.

It was frightening and sobering to know that Daniil had been occupying the same space as I was. He could have crawled out and killed me in my sleep.

All those late-night sounds. That could've been him. The cops believed he had been surviving on eating the very insects he collected, but what if he'd come out to raid my kitchen, too.

I was actively working on a lawsuit against Olga.

* * *

Retrospective: Florne's Ghost

By Emil Pellim

"Living room, dying room, bedroom, sleepless
Late night, moonlight kisses my sisters
Bunk beds, sheer drapes, windows to wonders
We stare out and wonder why peace is beyond us"

"Homebaked" Verse Three, Florne/Ridicule-us Records

It has been twenty years to the day since Florne's sophomore single entered the Swedish charts directly at number one. After the lukewarm reception of "Love/Violence," Florne was given a second chance by her managers at Ridicule-us with "Homebaked." It exceeded all expectations and peaked not only locally but across most of Western Europe (pockets of Balkan success followed). Within weeks of release, "Homebaked" achieved gold status, which transmuted through time to platinum.

"Homebaked" features a mere three standard synthesizer-composed layers (on a Roland JP-8000), otherwise entirely made up of sampled recordings of ambient sounds. Two hundred twenty-four to be exact; it pushed the limit of the number of simultaneous tracks of digital audio workstations at the time. Ambient sampling was a common musical technique for her local contemporaries. Florne nevertheless advanced the trend to a place of her own by the mere number. An album's worth of samples in a single.

The samples used include the sound of a comforter being dragged off a bed, rain dripping from a gutter into mud, a television newscast as heard beyond two walls, a shaving razor tapped against ceramic, a cigarette igniting. And, of course, the one that seeded the infamy of

"Homebaked"—the barely audible babble of the waters of Lake Karin, the host of Florne's waterfront childhood home.

The first specific mention of the ghost's echo we could unearth is from a recorded broadcast by FMusik.

Transcript of recorded call, courtesy of FMusik
(*translated to English by Dominika P.*)

[*call starts*]

Caller: That song you just played—

DJ: "Homebaked?" What a tune, isn't it!

Caller: Whatever it's called. It plays every damn day on my drive to work.

DJ: Well, lady, it's a popular song. People request it.

Caller: That's fine, that's fine. But I think your recording is messed up.

DJ: Messed up how?

Caller: There's a faint sound. Like a distant scream or something similar. Maybe a minute from the end.

DJ: Are you sure it wasn't the noise of the city outside of your car?

Caller: Sure as the Sunday blues. I keep turning down the radio when I hear it. I roll down the windows. I listen to the cityscape. Nothing. The third or fourth time, I realized it was always the same song I was turning down.

DJ: Our recording is straight from the company. It's probably one of the samples used for the song. I haven't noticed it though.

Caller: Take it as you will.

[*call ends*]

The call was a flare attracting the attention of young people all over the city, their hearing most capable of picking up the high-pitched frequency over all the other layers of the track. Within the month, loudmouthed school-aged clubgoers started to duet to the scream. Wait for the exact moment it was heard and produce a twin with their beer-stench breaths. This author is embarrassed to say they've screamed the scream themselves once upon a time. Some DJs tried to remove the song from rotation, but requests were persistent and management would strongarm them into inserting it back into their sets, lest patrons tipsy-turvy over to a club next door.

As any other silly fad, it too would have died down within a few dawns had it not been for Florne's visit to FMusik two months later. She was scheduled to perform an acoustic version of "Homebaked" on DJ Rasmus' show, "Voices & Vices."

Following her beautiful raspy rendition with notes so low they swept the floor, Rasmus as usual conducted a mini-interview. He asked her slightly sordid questions about the song, the album, the quick fame, the men and women in her life. Like the little shit he was, he bridged risqué topic after topic as a way of surveying the perimeter of Florne's personal boundaries. In a rare error, he mismeasured and crossed over, causing her to become curt in her replies. Rasmus could sense the soiled mood to be unrecoverable and hurried to wrap things up, unknowingly asking his most important question as an afterthought.

Transcript of Voices & Vices Episode 226, courtesy of FMusik
(*translated to English by Dominika P.*)

[*timestamp: 19:24:56*]

Rasmus: Thanks for taking the time to—

Florne: Yeah, sure.

Rasmus: As a goodbye to your fans, would you mind giving us your best "Homebaked" scream? Just not too close to the microphone, or you'll scare an old lady to death somewhere.

Florne: My what?

Rasmus: You know... "We stare out and wonder why peace is beyo-*aaaaghh*-nd us."

[*silence*]

Rasmus: The scream, the one that everyone's been doing at the clubs.

Florne: I haven't been to a club in months. I've recently come back from tour. In Germany, no one was screaming at me. At most, they were gently swaying.

Rasmus: But... the sample you used, why a scream? Does it mean anything?

Florne: I didn't use a scream for a sample. Some of them were altered, modulated for mood. Maybe it's one of those, and you're probably mishearing.

Rasmus: Maybe. Well, thank you again for being here.

Florne: No probl—

Rasmus [*louder*]: "We stare out and wonder why peace is beyo-*AAAAGHH*-nd us."

[*timestamp: 19:26:12*]

Specifics of the policework have not been made public, but, by piecing together information from various articles in the days following, we can establish a general timeline. Florne had gone home and listened to the master of her track, and heard the scream, quite late to the party. She says she had replayed the song hundreds of times while producing it without noticing; her ears were so fixated on perfecting the intentional sounds she had arranged that they had completely overlooked the intruding scream.

The scream, occurring at the end of verse three, was embedded in the sample of the aforementioned ambient sounds of Lake Karin. Florne determined this by listening to the individual source files of all three samples playing in the song at that time (the lake, a bead curtain swinging open, and a houseplant's leaves dragging against a wall).

She extracted the exact date and time from the file's metadata and provided them to authorities. Detectives modeled the sound propagation of a sample of scream volumes, applying fluid mechanics. By pitting these virtual screams against the real for comparison, they determined that the scream was likely emitted two to three hundred meters away and had surfed the waters of the lake before becoming a faint whisper in Florne's microphone.

Theo Wilhelm, a nine-year-old boy, had been declared missing by his parents, Francisca and Jacob, just four hours after the time of recording.

For their yearly family vacation, the Wilhelm family had rented a waterfront property occupying the shore opposite the lake from Florne's home. Jacob claims he had gone to get breakfast for the family, leaving Theo and Francisca in the room. Francisca says she woke up and went to bathe, leaving Theo asleep in bed. When washed, dried, and primped, she returned and found the room empty. She has no recollection of hearing the front entrance opening, though that's to be expected with a running shower behind a closed bathroom door.

Months of directionless searches and airwave pleas by the parents and police had produced no leads. With the discovery of the recording and the results of the analysis, the police had a new trail to follow. They organized a thorough inspection of the shores of the lake at the distance derived from the models. The initial conditions had been narrowed to reflect the voice box of a boy of nine, constraining results fairly tightly.

It was a junior policewoman on her trial period who found the first clue, later promoted for her efforts. At a particular spot twenty meters from the epicenter of interest, the shore of the lake ascended to a mild cliff. Only a meter or so separated the water's surface from the cliff's surface. It was not an intimidating drop; one could conceive of a child deciding to dive from the top.

In the water below, however, a pewter-colored rock barely poked above the water's surface. Its color was like camouflage against the reflection of the cliff and sky above. The policewoman had spotted it by pure chance, her sharp eye catching on an incongruity, and her intuition sensing danger in the rock's placement.

As a next step, law enforcement commissioned a team of divers to sift the area around and look for more concrete clues, if any. The search was slow—divers on record say that the freshwater vegetation had braided a carpet of roots on the lake floor that was draining to parse. Its shadowy mazes stole the surface light, and formed phantom contours that looked like things but weren't.

Still, on the second morning, a diver found something real tangled into one of the below-surface roots—a human jaw. The mostly permanent teeth embedded within, coupled with the relatively small size of the jaw, implied a child between seven and eleven. The bone fragment was sent to a lab for analysis to determine whether it belonged to Theo.

Due to a backlog at the forensics lab, the test could not be carried out for another week—by which point it was made redundant by the consecutive discovery. The continued efforts of the divers helped locate Theo's body forty meters from the rock, two days after his jaw was found. The currents had carried the boy to his final resting place, where his legs had caught the side of a submerged log and anchored him.

The diver, who happened upon Theo, eventually quit his job and diving altogether. He was open and honest with his reasons—the image of Theo had taken a stronghold in his mind and he could never shed it.

Quote by Samson Lyttle; excerpt from his interview with Channel Channel
(*aired one week post-discovery*)

"There was only so much skin left on the face, the

rest looked like it was eaten away or rotted and dissolved in the depths. Like old furniture that needs reupholstered. His head bobbed up and down, a buoy in the lakewater underdraft. This very movement was what initially caught my eye. I swam in his direction and could see him more clearly as I approached. His entire chin was gone. His face was stretched into a gaping smile. It was the face of death, laughing at the living. I know that in my own bones. It felt like swimming toward my doom, toward the arms of the beyond."

***

Investigators concluded that Theo had wandered away from the hotel room while his mother showered, and attempted an innocent jump off the cliff-like lake bank. Unfortunately, the rock below was near-impossible to notice. The working theory was that he tried to belly-flop into the water and landed on his chin. Despite the low height, the angle of impact was sufficient to completely tear off his jaw and send it floating separately from the rest of his body.

The police force's medical specialists said they hoped he had died instantly, but they likely knew better, ameliorating the potentials to placate the parents. If he had gone quickly, the scream on "Homebaked" would have been one of glee from hopping into the water—not a guttural wail of pain.

Being gentle was a courtesy the police could not be sure they should extend. Most disappearances and deaths were the wrongdoings of the parents themselves—chance accidents are a less common threat to children than their own blood and beginnings. In this case though, there were no witnesses or evidence to link parent to peril, and the death had to be ruled accidental or else the case would become as cold as the winter waters of Karin.

When it comes to pop culture, trends live and die with locomotive momentum. The managers of Ridicule-us Records spent a pretty sum to keep the number one spot for as long as possible, but fighting a decline in popularity is like propping a collapsing castle with a palm. "Sesame Seeds" by Keila L was first to dethrone "Homebaked" locally, for one week, then "Sad, Sad Boys" by Mini, Maxi & Hefti took over for two.

But that was all before the body. In an entertainment industry improbability, "Homebaked's" chart slip was reversed, and it once again shot up to the top. How could it not? Every radio station and TV channel played it, mostly as context for news stories capitalizing on Theo Wilhelm's death. An infamous revival.

Lake Karin had been peaceful as all of Sweden prior to the discovery. It is now too, but in those first months after Theo was found, the lake became an attractor for local and not-so-local youth. It flooded with people. Rumors were better than advertisements when it came to pulling people into this otherwise unremarkable locale. Everyone wanted to see Theo's ghost.

Whether you believe in ghosts or not (we, the staff, do not), Theo's has an attributable death count. Three.

Tomasz Ptak was first to face the phantom and not live to tell about it. His best friend Jan Konopka, also studying economics in Sweden at the time, relayed the details of the supposed encounter in an issue of "Pop-Corny," in their native Poland. He witnessed the death of his friend firsthand, filtered through the lens of seven unfiltered ciders.

Segment from Interview with Konopka, Pop-Corny, Issue 43
(translated to English by Patrycja G.)

Jan: Oh man. We were swimming, right? Just flopping around. Like fish, we were.

Pop-C: So, what happened? What happened to Tomasz?

Jan: Oh man, oh man. So, just fish, flopping, you know? We were just having fun. That's all we wanted.

Pop-C: How did the fun end?

Jan: We were just floating, laughing. Farting in the water and pushing fartwater toward each other with scooped hands, you know? And then, oh man! I heard it clear as if over earbuds. A scream like sizzling static. Like the one in the song, but loud like fuck.

Pop-C: Where was it emanating from?

Jan: It wasn't coming from anywhere, it was just everywhere. Like, beamed into my ears.

Pop-C: Do you think Tomasz heard it too?

Jan: Oh man, no man! I don't think it. I know it. We were both upstream salmon—thrashing about. Trying to shake that sound out as if it were water logged in our ear canals.

Pop-C: So, Tomasz was still alive at that time?

Jan: Yes, of course he was alive. My boy is an excellent swimmer. Was. We were both on the team in high school. Anyway, man, we wiggled and shook, but the scream deposited itself into our brains.

Pop-C: How did Tom—

Jan: Like... my brain was mush. I could barely focus on staying afloat.

Pop-C: And Tomasz?

Jan: Tomasz was a better swimmer. A tepid lake was breakfast, lunch, and dinner for him.

Pop-C: So wh—

Jan: He took him. Man, oh man. The dead little shit took him. He wrapped himself around Tomasz like seaweed, like a whirlpool. It was a shadow at first, but then a little hand reached out from below the surface. It grabbed his jaw and pried it open like a vice. Until it was so wide it could swallow a billiards ball whole. Don't interrupt, please. Don't interrupt! I see you have something to say, man. But let me say mine. His mouth was pried so wide it turned into a cavern. Water seeped into it and flooded it. Tomasz' gurgling scream was pale compared to the one we heard seconds prior. But it was his, and it was his last.

Pop-C: Had Tomasz had anything to drink before you went swimming?

Jan: Nothing, man! Like, three beers and three ciders, tops. Barely a drop. We've swam championships on more.

***

A single day later, Theo's ghost claimed the second in the series of three. In the case of LZ [*initials changed to protect the privacy of a toddler as per local law - Ed.*], we cannot blame alcohol or teenage antics. His parents, who should have perhaps kept their son under more stringent supervision, did not commit a sin egregious enough to be crucified over—just casual carelessness.

The two men, vacationing visitors to the lake, had been watching the news while LZ played with toy trucks on the couch in the same room. They had arrived only an hour or two earlier, after a long drive from neighboring Norway. One of the fathers had grown up a chalk's chuck away from the lake and was brought back by boyhood memories he hoped to remake like an old movie, this time starring his son. This family was not the sort of spirit seekers that saturated most other rentals in the area at the time.

Exhaustion from travel paired with the puffy pillows had put the couple to sleep. Neither of them noticed their son sneaking out of the rented villa. LZ's next known location was the elevated bank where little Theo was thought to have jumped into the jaws of death.

There was a slew of swimming spectators this time. When interviewed later, each unfortunate by-swimmer recounted the same story—they saw a toddler boy standing at the edge of the cliff, quiet and intense and bound in a trance. Then, he made a few false starts into a run and dive, as if dissatisfied with his footing.

The third or fourth try was true, and he dove off of the ledge, arms reaching forward. His chin smashed into the very rock that Theo was thought to have lost a jaw to. Although the jump was almost expertly executed, the jaw did not detach in this case—instead, it hung loose within the flesh like change in a coin purse, dancing in the currents as people pulled at the body to float him ashore. Assured that the boy was beyond being helped, they waited for an ambulance not to save him, but so they could collect the news and body and deliver it to whichever relatives would be blaming themselves for the incident for all eternity.

Society simply needed an explanation for this behavior, even if in truth it could have been as random as the roll of a die—fate's realized intrusive thought. So, one such was concocted by experts. LZ's parents had fallen asleep while watching a local news channel that was airing a segment on Theo's death at the time. The broadcast included crudely-rendered 3D simulations of Theo's jump with graphics no better than consoles two generations ago. The animations were imports from overseas news channels that had capitalized on the peculiar story.

Monkey see, monkey do. The toddler took the animations as an instruction manual, found his way out while his daddies slept, and supposedly tried to recreate the trajectory he had seen on screen.

Bulgarian tourist Gergana Paunova was third to walk the ghost's plank. Her co-traveler and very recent husband, Naum, had to bring home from his own honeymoon not souvenirs but a casket. "Homebaked" was the pair's wedding song. Naum's father Toma, so happy for his son's union with a highly intelligent and kind woman who would hopefully reason out the wrinkles in his son's sometimes immature personality, had gifted the trip to them.

In an interview with Bulgarian specialty program "Neuznavaema

Vselena" (Unfathomable Universe), appearing as devastated as his son, Toma lamented the loss of his daughter-in-law. His tears dripped onto the blurry photograph that his own son had captured.

Segment from interview with Paunovi Family, Neuznavaema Vselena, Ep. 104
(*translated to English by Anastasia T.*)

Toma: She was a soul that could embarrass a saint. Naum was undeservedly lucky, winning life's lottery while loitering around.

Naum: Stiga be, tatko. ["Quiet/enough, father" - *An.T*]

[*Toma places a hand heavy with comfort on his son's shoulder*]

Naum: Yes, it's true, Gergana was a goddess.

Toma: The devils of the world can't have that. A beacon of light like her has to be extinguished, or they'll melt in her shine like moths made of sugar.

[*Naum smacks the tear-smeared photograph he is holding; the edge of the thick photopaper springing back to shape after*]

Naum: The thing that killed Gergana is right here, staring dead into the lens like a gloating ghoul.

[*Naum uses his finger to trace an elliptical outline around a blurry background shape*]

Naum: Just look at its mouth. It's an abyss. I could fit a fist in it. Both. Oh, how I would like to get my fists on this phantom. This fucker.

Interviewer [*off-screen*]: I understand you took

this photograph yourself? And don't curse, this airs at seven.

Naum: I did. And it's on the negative too—this isn't the first printed copy, if that's what you're gonna try and get at.

Interviewer [*off-screen*]: What I wanted to ask was, why was your reaction upon seeing such a thing to pick up a camera and take a photograph instead of helping Gergana?

[*Naum becomes visibly agitated*]

Naum: That's not how it happened, and you know that. Don't be asking stupid questions!

Interviewer [*off-screen*]: Ami togava? ["Well, then what?" - *An.T*]

Naum: She wanted me to take a photo. To show the family later, show them we were having fun, you understand me. They paid for the trip after all—no small feat for one of us, living in the Europe that ain't really Europe. They sacrificed so much to get us to the lake. A typical weekend for a Westerner, once or less in a lifetime for a Balkan, you know?

[*the person conducting the interview sounds sympathetic but also short of time and needs to move things along*]

Interviewer [*off-screen*]: Are you saying the capture was serendipitous, not intentional?

Naum: Yes, yes. Through the viewfinder, everything seemed normal, or at the very least, too tiny to tell otherwise. But as I dropped the camera from my face, I noticed Gergana struggling to stay afloat.

Interviewer [*off-screen*]: Did you see anything

else?

Naum: Just people, lots of other people around. They all noticed too, and rushed toward Gergana, got there way before me given they were closer. There was one man, Hugo—he still texts me to check up on me, bless his brain—he had grabbed her and was already dragging her out when I got to her. We both pulled against the resistance of the water that seemed like it wanted to keep her. I got her out as fast as possible. Not fast enough. Not fast enough...

Interviewer [*off-screen*]: I apologize in advance if you find my next question insensitive. Do you think, with all the commotion and the state of panic you were in, you could have failed to notice something?

Naum: Stop chewing straw and spit it out. What are you asking?

Interviewer [*off-screen*]: Have you heard of the Sliemen family?

Naum: Who?

***

Sure, the Sliemen theory is all speculation. But speculating is just the act of trying to make sense out of a dark stain of information, bringing it into focus through perspective. It is no more absurd than interpreting the dark figure in the photograph behind Gergana Paunova as a ghost.

At the particular time of Gergana's last breaths, the lake was reportedly full and brimming as it had been for weeks post-ghost. A local family, collectively called the Sliemens after the eldest member, Ebbe Sliemen, were enjoying the cool waters of Karin same as everyone else. It could be considered a special occasion for them. Ebbe was normally confined to a care facility, his own facilities failing in recent years. On a rare day out, his family decided to take him to the lake so the waters and breezes could soothe his mind.

The grandchildren fought over a handheld with the newest Mario game. The mother re-read the first few pages of a book she liked to false-start. The father dozed, covered by a hat. Whatever activities each of them was engaged in monopolized their attention. Collectively, they let Ebbe slip out of mind and out of sight. Into the water.

The Sliemens say that when Gergana's drowning struggles shook the beach, they looked in the general direction and there Ebbe was, a few feet behind the distressed girl. He was splashing up and down like an apple in a bobbing tub. Mom and dad Sliemen ran to retrieve Ebbe before his old muscles could fail to bob him back up one of these times. For them a priority over helping Gergana.

And they did get to him before he slipped, before he was forced to use his extinguished wing-arms to stay afloat. A task he would have failed for certain. This day of loss could have easily been a day of double-such. Ebbe was doused in joy when they reached him. A toothless smile as big as a yawn sat stupidly on his wrinkled face. Ebbe's son and daughter-in-law succeeded in dragging him out with no incident.

In fact, they both say they had forgotten the incident until they saw the photograph that Gergana's husband had taken. It was published in all the local tabloids. According to them, the image caught Ebbe mid-bop, with his lower lip submerged just below the surface and his toothless mouth open wide into a gummy, gleeful smile. The water reflected his mouth, and when combined with the original, it looked like a boa with a jaw big enough to swallow a swallow whole. The photographed ghost-blur was, according to the family, an old man just shy of a ghost himself but not quite there yet.

All in all, Karin claimed in a summer as many as it had in the past two hundred years combined. This is no endorsement of the ghost's existence. For someone to succumb to death and doom, a living person would have to be there in the first place. And such were the statistics—

in the decades preceding the fame of the lake, only the few families long-settled on the shores swam its waters.

Their feet were accustomed to every rise and fall of the relief of the lake bottom. A map charted in their minds, and an instinct inherited from a lengthy lineage of great-to-the-nth grandparents who populated the lake's perimeter. The arriving masses attracted by "Homebaked" lacked this history, and a predictably small fraction of them perished.

The lake's tourism waned proportionally to the song's popularity. Youth and yonder swarmed to locales that were more actual. More central to pop culture and more capable of garnering interest from friends upon seeing photos and hearing stories.

"Homebaked" fell out of the collective conscience of Europe. It only made sparse appearances on shows that highlighted retro music, shows whose loose criterium for retro would include still-edible food from a rarely-cleaned fridge. Last year, last decade—equal sentences to a song hanging by an invisible, ghostly thread.

Florne's career ended just as unceremoniously. First came the whimpers that were her third and fourth singles ("For All the Names" and "Murder by Manners"). I'd like to point out that our own publication gave both of them five out of five ecstasy tablets when we reviewed them back in their day. We also accurately (and with great disappointment over it) predicted they'd fail to achieve commercial success—not just for lacking a ghost as a mascot but for challenging the listener with difficult topics expressed with almost-subliminal subtlety. The same perky ears that easily picked up Theo's voice were deaf to Florne's.

A second, unnamed album with a single released single ("Undergrowth") was the straw that broke the label's bank. The song debuted somewhere in the very extended tails of the local charts and dropped off completely in a week. Even the music video for the song is more recognizable than the song itself, having been directed by famed director Michael Gandrey and pioneering camera techniques like rotating zoom and unfollow focus.

The album, which was completed and mastered and had its first run already pressed, was delayed indefinitely when Ridicule-us Records petitioned for bankruptcy. Warner narrowly lost to Universal in the auction for the release rights. Universal sat on the album for five years, until Florne won a lawsuit that forced them to release the rights back to the artist. By that point, she lacked the clout that would attract another, more daring label to give it a try.

So, the story ends. The previously popular girl is crowded out from the minds of people by all the new thoughts and feelings and songs arriving day by day. I say this with no pointed criticism—I'm guilty of it myself. It had been at least fifteen years since I thought of this artist called Florne; you know, the one who had a couple of good songs, the one with the scream.

This very recently changed, and she came back to life—at least to mine.

I was supposed to review the intimate concert by "The Driller Killers" at Leon's Palace last Tuesday. Imagine my surprise when the bar owner announced, five minutes before the set time, that due to unforeseen circumstances, they were being replaced by a "local talent by the name of Florne."

Later, I found out she was renting the room above the bar, and the manager had asked her to play to prevent at least a minority of the ticket holders from asking for a full refund. The stage was hers as an absolute last resort.

She walked out and quietly set up her loop pedal to no cheers from the crowd that would indicate recognition. Their drunken chatter dulled little in volume. My own recognition, even upon hearing the name, set in slowly. My mind was trying to place the name and face together, like seeing a forgotten classmate from high school. Or was it university?

When all was ready, Florne assumed her position in front of the microphone. She pressed her foot against the pedal to start recording the first layer of the song, and then let out a breathy low tone that ignited the embers of memory in me, and quieted the rest of the crowd into awed attention.

Song after unknown song tickled my feelings. Some were joy, some were torture; all were pure power. The songwriting and delivery felt familiar and yet unfathomably different from the Florne I knew decades ago. These tunes were like children with different genetic material but raised with the same morals and ideals.

The sonic complexity of "Love/Violence" and "Homebaked" was replaced by lo-fi, live-recorded layers numbering in single digits. Florne's message lost nothing to simplicity—she seasoned her raw ingredients solely with salt and pepper, using no heavy spices that could overwhelm the palate.

At the end of the night, I drooped from the exhaustion that accompanied feeling the kind of feelings that Florne had brought to share. The crowd around me felt the burden too. The music had lulled us into quietly dreaming along with her, even in nightmares, and we were drained to the bottom. Like a scuttering mouse making off with stolen goods from the pantry, Florne hurried backstage immediately, her final note lingering in the air.

I left quickly as well, to beat the rush at coat check and the confusion on the street over which identical charcoal car belongs to which ride-sharer. The phone app gave me five minutes for a joint. As soon as I lit it, I felt a tapping on my right shoulder. "Can I have a drag?" I puff-puff-passed. "You can have two, if I can have an interview."

Interview with Florne, conducted December 21 at Dark Donkey Cafe

Me: Thank you so much for meeting me this chilly morning.

Florne: Don't be fooled, it's all at the prospect of a free breakfast.

Me: I'll jump into it. I'm not trying to butter you up

like a breakfast croissant—but the show last week wrecked me.

Florne: I apologize for the ruin.

Me: It's quite all right. All that fell were barricades.

Florne: For the better, then.

Me: For the better.

Florne: Ugh! I'm actually a little nervous.

Me: I'm sure you've given interviews aplenty.

Florne: Not in a long while. It's funny. As a young girl hungry for success, I would jump on every opportunity. To stay top of mind, you know? But "Homebaked" blew up, and with time, interviews became trite, a thing to avoid. The same inane questions time after time. Then people stopped coming around, stopped asking. And all of a sudden, I wanted to speak, but there was no one listening.

Me: If a one-hit-wonder speaks and there's no one around to hear it, does it make a sound?

Florne [*laughing*]: HEY!

Me: Sorry, sorry. I am, of course, kidding.

Florne: It's not an issue at all. A time-and-a-half ago, I would have been sensitive on the topic. The feelings I felt when I first lost fame could fill a bucket, with overflow.

Me: I can only imagine. But you must have been set for life, right? Just the royalties from all those crime programs about Theo's death would feed you for eternity, I'm sure.

Florne: Oh, the royalties—just another feeling in that bucket. Every channel filmed their own special about Theo. The song I had sweated over played from TVs across the nation, and you know what I got out of it? A big, fat nothing. Wasn't in my contract.

Me: Haven't laws changed since then? Can't you sue?

Florne: Sure, but I can't squeeze fish juice out of coral. The money's been long spent by record executives and companies that have gone bankrupt. I'd just be spending money I don't have on legal fees.

Me: That's rough, I'm sorry.

Florne: Sånt är livet.

Me: How are you making a living? I haven't seen your live shows advertised at any of the venues around town, and I visit them lots to review artists. Are you still recording? I couldn't find anything on the net.

Florne [*laughing*]: Ever since Florne Furniture opened in Stockholm, they have dominated the first pages of search results—even my name is no longer actual. But, to answer your question, Emil, I do make new music. Haven't always, though. I've neglected the therapy of creation for years at a time in the past. But now I'm on a wave and I'm riding it and it's working, and I'll focus on the breeze and not question or predict how long it will last.

Me: If the songs you played the other night are newly composed, it definitely is working. Can we expect an album anytime soon?

Florne: I feel like albums are a thing of my past. Barely, [laughs] I had only one album officially released. Anyway, the new songs I've been writing don't have a common enough theme to join into a unified record. They're all talking—loudly at that—just not to each other.

Me: What about EPs? Singles?

Florne: I did try selling songs individually online for a buck a tune, but it felt trivial to ask for that. So, I switched to a free-to-download approach with a link to donate via PatronizeMe. On that note, if you search my name and you go to—I think I'm on page eight of the results now—you'll find the site where I post them for free.

*[Click **here** to listen to Florne's new music - Ed.]*

Me: I'll be sure to check them out.

Florne: Thank you for listening in advance, then.

Me: The pleasure will be mine, I am sure. So that's how modern-day artists sustain themselves? Donations?

Florne: I'm sure it's not impossible if your voice—and I don't mean vocals—resonates with enough people. Mine seems quiet, like Theo's scream. Maybe with time, people will notice it too. But not yet. So far, donations total a whopping two weeks' worth of groceries.

Me: How do you meet the basic needs of life?

Florne: It's been a struggle. I don't mean to imply I'm going hungry or homeless, but that I'm engaged in a balancing act that I've only recently found to be close to equilibrium—the right amount of menial labor in exchange for the right amount of necessities, with the occasional luxury when I really need to feel like a princess and not a pauper. But most importantly, with enough emotional energy left over to make music on my days off. Without that, I'd be a vampire—working solely to feed myself with no greater purpose behind devouring.

Me: What kind of manual labor?

Florne: I work at the fruit market next door to Leon's Palace. Minimum wage, but at least we're in one of the only countries where that means something. And

I live right above Leon's Palace too, on the cheap, no commute that way either. Alex, the manager, said I could stay there for small change as long as I fix the audio equipment downstairs when he needs it. So, I do my fruity duty at the market twenty hours a week, eat a lot of rotting pears and apples about to be thrown out, and try to spend little on anything else except time on music. I'm saving for some new equipment to evolve my sound too, so I can mold it closer to how I really feel. It's like constantly trying for a rounder circle. Can't ever get it perfect, but can always be closer.

Me: That's quite a feat here. This city is not so livable on a grocery clerk's salary.

Florne: Nowadays, it's not much more livable on most salaries. Nor livable on a mind drained by work and left with nothing to give.

Me: No, I suppose not. Has it been a difficult adjustment? Going from a period when you would have been recognized by anyone in the country, to working at a market and making music in a room above a dive bar?

Florne: Of course it has been.

Me: Can you be more specific?

Florne: I was both lucky and unlucky, in that I had a very calm childhood with no major trauma. My grandparents were alive well into my twenties, my parents and sisters loving, my house cozy, my country mostly moral. The value of pain, and the strength that can be derived from it, had evaded me. I hadn't learned the techniques to cope with life as it really is, only the lacquered version of it.

Me: Yet your early music still carries a certain level of sadness and melancholy within.

Florne: It does, doesn't it? I guess even contented

existence does. When making "Homebaked," I used every nostalgic sound I could think of, truly believing they represented what shaped me as a person. But the universe knew better than my young, naive self—knew that for more than a decade following, I would be much more forcefully shaped by what was lacking in my childhood than that which was present. Namely, pain and loss. I feel like that's why it inserted Theo's dying scream into the song—to supplement my experience and teach me something that life had failed to do. I was babied by life, but reared by death.

Me: That's an interesting way to look at it [*laughs*]. I must say, you seem to be in a peaceful place now.

Florne: Peace is a strange concept. I used to sing, "We stare out and wonder why peace is beyond us..." Now I know better—peace is not beyond me, nor anyone else—it's just not permanent. I used to think peace was a destination, but it is in fact a recurring pitstop on the road to the only destination. Whenever you encounter it, stay there 'til it disappears and leaves you with all the road under your feet again.

Me: Grim thoughts for a grim winter morning.

Florne: You think so? I would consider them hopeful.

Me: It's all in the eye of the beholder, I suppose. Ah! Unfortunately, the clock behind you reminds me that it's time to wrap up, as much as I am enjoying the chat.

Florne: See? Time ticks quietly behind us to the end of everything.

Me: Now I'm gonna be looking over my shoulder all day, for time. Can't let it get me!

Florne: Watch your back. [*makes ticking clock noises*]

Me[*laughing*]: Before we bid adieu, are there any parting words of wisdom you'd like to leave for fans, future musicians, or maybe even amateur ghost hunters?

"Hectic strangers in dirty fast fashions
Hurry past peace in rushed legions
Peace, the privilege of pursued passion
Starve, fit the gap to creative regions"

"Peace-wise Function" Verse One, Florne/Self-Produced

* * *

7734

By Ryan Benson

Roberta Henson hunched over the snowmobile's handlebars and forced every last bit of speed from the machine. The Arctic wind burned the skin surrounding her exposed mouth, but she dared not slow down. She'd maintained a constant frenetic rate since fleeing the *Lady Dawn*—a desperate dot of black streaking across the desolate white landscape.

Henson only moved her body when wiping her goggles or peering over each shoulder. These peeks allowed views of the extra gas tanks she'd fastened to the rear of the vehicle. Past the fuel, only kilometers of white nothingness lay behind her. The *Lady Dawn*'s crew had no way to follow her. Yet, the primal dread of a prey animal filled her gut. The terror persisted despite reassuring herself it was her imagination. A land, so barren and devoid of anything, must lack evil as sure as it seemed to lack anything resembling good. But she welcomed invisible dangers compared to what infected the ship—that damn number: 7734.

During her rearview check, the snowmobile hit an upturned shard of ice. Henson lifted from the seat. Only the white-knuckled grip on the handlebars prevented her from tumbling to the ground. With more than a little trepidation, Henson did the unthinkable and slowed her flight to a stop. Tendrils of steam escaped her lips, followed by a torrent of curses. All but one of the gas containers lay in the snow, bleeding dark fluid. In seconds, the vast openness had transformed into a wide-open prison.

She patted her pant and coat pockets until she found the soothing shape of the revolver. Now somewhat calmer, Henson surveyed the land. Snow wisps formed phantom people before they blew apart seconds later. She maneuvered closer to the black pools and, in the absence of duct tape, ruled both gas cans unusable. Would the remaining fuel last until she reached some form of civilization? Could she have made it even under optimum conditions?

Her plan had holes, but it was a plan. With a little luck, she'd find a government research base or an Inuit village before she froze, or the gas ran out. Henson bounced her knee and stared at the horizon. If only those squabbling fools onboard the *Lady Dawn* hadn't forced her to take matters into her own hands.

Henson bore no hard feelings. The hysteria among her fellow scientists concerning 7734 would have surprised her if she hadn't experienced it firsthand. Stress could unnerve the steadiest mind, including hers.

The discord between her colleagues on the ship had seemed impossible when they departed the Institute in Hawaii. Two months ago, the shrinking polar caps opened up new and unexplored areas for the Institute's research flagship, the *Lady Dawn*. Although built for visiting more temperate climates, the craft could now sail farther north without fear of icebergs. The newly tenured Henson jumped at the opportunity. Among the most attractive dive targets was the *USS Buchanan* of the "doomed" 1868 Thomas expedition to the North Pole. The nineteenth-century vessel had never returned and was assumed to rest in a deep icy grave.

Only one faculty member pushed back against Henson. Her former advisor John Bass argued the expedition was doomed to failure. Still, she won out with the department chair and funding committee. To Henson's surprise, Bass arranged for him and his people to accompany the expedition.

Henson held high hopes for the trip. She had done her homework, secured the grant funding, and mapped the dive sites. Sunshine and favorable currents brought the *Lady Dawn* to its destination days ahead of schedule. Good fortune, however, vanished the day they reached their target location. Water testing instruments malfunctioned, giving impossibly high and low temperature readings. All means of electronic communication failed by nightfall. Around midnight, Henson sat in the instrument room. Anxious scientists checking equipment crowded around her. She rested her head in her hands and rubbed her temples.

A loud click of the tongue behind Henson startled her from her mental frustration. Bass scowled, running his hand over the thick silver beard matching his combed hair. "Are you sure you trained your team in the use of the equipment? The mismanagement of this little journey is costing the Institute a lot of money and costing me a lot of time."

Without looking at Bass, Henson scooted by him, turning herself to avoid the man's protruding gut. "The quality of my research AND my people is exactly why the chair awarded me the use of the *Lady Dawn*." She needed some good news. "Any luck, Chambers?"

A lanky man stood up from behind a desk. "I know we set up everything correctly if that's what you're asking." The postdoctoral student pushed his shaggy brown hair from his eyes and flashed a smile. Henson's anxiety thawed, though failed to melt entirely. She had hired Chambers for his background in meteorology, but their chemistry had since made him invaluable. Midnight brainstorming and tandem coffee runs had made the expedition possible. *Batman and Robin*.

"Always with the jokes." Bass exhaled and shook his head.

"Your man Meachem can't diagnose the problem either." Henson pointed at a blond-haired man furrowing his brow and fiddling with a tangle of wires. She hoped no one saw her finger trembling with resentment. Frustration begged her to say more, but her respect for the older scientist stilled her tongue.

"Meachem," said Bass, but the man continued plugging and unplugging electrical cords. "Meachem!"

Meachem popped to attention. "Yes, Dr. Bass?"

"In my many years leading projects for the Institute, have we ever approached this level of disaster?"

"No, sir," Meachem said, and after a nod from Bass, he returned to his tangle.

Henson remembered back when Bass acted nothing but friendly and helpful. The hostility between the two emerged as her career rocketed off, and his status sank so far they would need to raise another expedition to find it. The antipathy tore at her. She tried to remain civil, and he smiled enough when they conversed, but only with his mouth, never his eyes. No matter how Bass behaved, Henson could not shake the belief that she owed him for her spot at the Institute. The hope of a successful collaboration between her and Bass now seemed naive.

"We should sail back to port," said Bass. "The ship is deaf and blind to the world. We could sink, and no one would be the wiser."

Henson folded her arms across her chest to keep them from shaking. "If we leave now, another group with more intestinal fortitude could swoop in."

Both she and Bass knew if they found the *USS Buchanan*, the Institute would be a household name. Henson cared little for fame except for the accompanying funding for her work. She had learned it was a different story for Bass. "After we find the *Buchanan*, you can pitch a show to Nat Geo or the History Channel."

Bass grunted. "I say we give it another forty-eight hours."

Henson winked at Chambers. "Yes, Dr. Bass. Let's do that."

After a few more hours of futility, they retired to their cabins. Sleep eluded Henson. An uneasy presence separate from fatigue descended upon her, like a shroud over her brain. The next morning, she remained in her quarters—and in her mind—to pour over nautical maps.

Chambers tried to coax her into joining him in the mess hall for breakfast. "It's just jitters."

"No." Henson fixated on her laptop. "Something is off."

"No one has ever tried a dive like this. Your inner critic will shut up when we find the *Buchanan*. Let's get the submersibles ready. I'm sure the tech guys will have the radio and the internet working by tomorrow."

"It's not anticipation or jitters." Henson looked up. The sight of

Chambers' smile caused her to pause for an instant longer than usual. She cleared her throat. "I feel like I'm in the middle of a boring dream seconds before the surreal nightmare begins."

"Come on," said Chambers. "Almost time for the first dive."

Despite her postdoc's enthusiasm, dive after dive revealed nothing. Henson's dreams lay dying, but to her amazement, she felt relief. If anything, she wished she could stomp the dreams to death. Euthanize them. After months of planning, all she wanted was off the ship.

Two days later, with no word to or from the outside world, Henson prepared to set sail for an Alaskan port. A self-satisfied Bass was already in his quarters, working on a new expedition proposal. However, on the final dive, one of the remote submersibles found the *Buchanan*. Cheers and celebration filled the room as Chambers placed a hand on Henson's shoulder. Tears welled up. Smiling, she allowed a single drop of liquid pride to trickle down her cheek as she pumped her fist.

"Let's find her crew and put them to rest," she said. "And would someone call Dr. Bass?" Henson smiled at Chambers. "I'd like his expert opinion on our find."

An hour later, Henson's pride withered as the sub's lights revealed an absence of both artifacts and corpses. The discovery threatened to produce little anthropological worth, save the ship itself. The smirk on Bass' face made Henson sick. To hide her disappointment, she focused on the screen.

Disorientation and nausea filled Henson. How could she come so far only to fail? She reached for the monitor's power button but stopped when a carving on the mast caught her attention. Leaning in closer, she realized the design marred every surface of the *Buchanan*. Engraved on the poles, deck, and railings was a number: 7734. Henson could not imagine how they missed it on previous dives and did not care. She had found her piece of heaven in this nineteenth-century graffitied ship. "Chambers, call Captain Arthur. Cancel the return to port."

Henson awoke early the next morning to a crew in disarray. Miles of white sheets replaced the sea. Overnight the ship had become ice-locked.

The captain disciplined the night watchmen, though they seemed as shocked as anyone. *Probably drunk or high.* Stranger still, Captain Arthur reported they no longer knew *where* they were stuck. The GPS gave error readings. Compass needles, both magnetic and gyroscopic, twirled like spinners on a board game. Latitude and longitude had ceased to exist.

Satellite phones and the internet remained inoperable, but radio silence ended. That afternoon, an excited Chambers burst into Henson's cabin. Panting, he pointed at his radio, now repeating a series of beeps.

"What is it?" said Henson. "A code?"

"It's not Morse code." Chambers caught his breath. "There are three beeps and then four. But it skips to seven beeps and repeats once before going back to three and four."

"No," said Henson. "Not three, four, seven, seven. It's seven, seven, three, four."

"What is that?"

"7734, like on the *Buchanan*."

Silence reigned between them until Captain Arthur's voice cut in over the intercom. "Dr. Henson?"

"Yes?"

"You requested that I alert you of any changes to the communication blackout. We are picking up a pattern of beeps on all radio bands."

Henson sensed Chambers staring at her for answers, but she could only shake her head. "Thank you, Captain."

After the radio transmission, the 7734 pattern seemed to appear all over the vessel. The crew and academics developed a compulsion to quantify everything on the ship. Like eager school children, they played macabre games of hide and seek with the digits.

7734 steps to traverse the ship.

7734 kilometers from Hawaii to their last known coordinates.

7734 weeks since the Thomas expedition first embarked on their journey.

These four numbers brought an undercurrent of weird to the expedition. Excitement masked obsession, like the fragrance of chemical cleaners over a lingering rotten odor.

Addled minds crept toward neurosis. Within a day, all computers failed, preventing any further dives. The bug seemed selective, first communications, then navigation, and now computers. What's next? Lights? *Heat?* Theories regarding the equipment malfunctions ran from a Russian computer virus to shifts in the magnetic poles. No single hypothesis could explain both electronic and compass failures.

Henson tried to dismiss the 7734 sickness as cabin fever and threw herself into her report. Instead of using her laptop, she wrote in a notebook as she had as an undergrad. Chambers lent her his battery-powered calculator for the data crunching. *Maybe I'll stay over in his quarters if the temperature continues to drop,* she thought. *It's closer to the boiler.*

Their chemistry had always been almost too good. It wouldn't be the first faculty and postdoc liaison at the Institute, but unlike some of her peers, *she* could keep it in her pants. Why sacrifice her career for a fling? For over a decade, lonely weekends and nights in front of her computer served as her social life. Did she now deserve the experiences she had denied herself all this time?

As if on cue, Henson heard Chambers yelling her name and knocking at her door. She unzipped her hoody to her breastbone and checked her hair in the mirror. Her brown eyes met those of her reflection, and Henson chuckled before zipping back up to her chin. Upon opening the door, she found the postdoc standing shirtless and covered in beads of sweat. A rush of warmth coursed through her body—until she noticed the red smears on his chest.

"Something bad happened," Chambers muttered as he stared through Henson.

"Bad?" Henson touched his slippery chest. She rubbed the viscous liquid between her fingers, before recoiling in disgust. "Is this blood?" She wiped her hand on her pants. "What the hell happened?"

"Meacham chewed the nose off of the ship's engineer." Chambers bit his own lower lip until it turned white.

"Meachem?" For a moment, her mouth hung agape as she attempted to understand. "What do you mean, 'bit his nose off?'" she crossed her arms across her chest. "This isn't funny."

"I mean Meachem used his teeth to remove another man's nose. The entire thing." A sick smile crossed his face as he slowly mimed pulling his nose off. "I could see the two nostril holes. Blood gushed everywhere." His breathing quickened, and the smile disappeared. "I tried to stop the bleeding with my shirt."

Henson's arms uncrossed and dropped to her sides. An awkward deadpan overpowered her will to scream or slam the door. "Why did Meachem bite him?"

"Who knows? Someone with a first aid kit took over. I'd been so busy with the engineer I forgot about Meachem." Chambers scanned the walls until his empty gaze made its way to the ceiling. "Couldn't have been more than three minutes, but he'd used the blood to write 7734 all over the room." The postdoc crossed both of his outstretched arms over his head in an arc. "All over."

"Oh, God," Henson whispered. The taste of bile filled her mouth. She had spent too much time in her quarters. What was happening to the crew?

A voice yelled down the hall. "Henson, I have to talk to you." Bass chugged toward them faster than she had ever seen him move.

"I know about Meachem," said Henson.

"What? No, not that." Bass shook his head. "There is a problem with the ship. The ice ruptured the hull, as I predicted."

Henson pushed Chambers into her quarters. "Stay here." Without another word, she slammed the door and took off through the dim corridors toward the bridge. Bass followed behind like a hungry dog.

Captain Arthur confirmed Bass' smug claims. Ice had torn a hole in the hull of the *Lady Dawn*. Even if they freed the ship, the boat would sink to the bottom of the frigid waters. Henson failed to draw more information from the captain. Arthur's attention drifted around the room as if searching for something. He soon stopped responding to questioning.

Henson grew impatient. "Bass, where is the first mate?" The older man only shrugged. She grabbed the public address microphone. "There will be an emergency meeting of everyone onboard. If you are not in the mess hall in half an hour, you'll spend the rest of the expedition in the brig."

Was there a brig? Henson sifted through her clouded thoughts. If nothing else, she could chain someone to a pipe in the boiler room.

"You too, Bass." She tossed the microphone at Bass, who fumbled and dropped it. "Thirty minutes."

Henson returned to her quarters to clean up Chambers. She found him standing near the porthole, looking out into the expanse. A vacant look covered his face as if his brain had boarded up his eyes and left town. *Like Captain Arthur,* thought Henson. Chambers' head cocked to the side, and his arms dangled like a marionette. She sat him on the bed while he fixed his view on the floor and moved his lips in a silent conversation. His body swayed to a song only he could hear.

The sheen of blood and sweat on Chambers entranced Henson, keeping her from noticing his silent monologue. Without realizing it, she found herself straddling him—no sign of the blood-induced bile in her mouth. The red fluid stirred something primal in her, not animalistic but primeval. Henson massaged his chest. Slick and warm, the blood created entwined sensations of joy and guilt in her gut.

She jumped off him and removed her hoody, winding her body as she imagined a woman would do when seducing a man. Henson would usually blush at the thought of letting any person, let alone her postdoc, see this side of her. *What am I doing?* The reflection in the mirror pulled her attention away from Chambers. *Not too bad for a nerd*, she thought. Henson unfastened her bra and turned back to her quarry.

Chambers, again looking straight through Henson, tapped his foot in a repeating pattern. "Chambers?" she said. The beat continued. "Don?"

The rhythm seemed familiar. A song? No. *The radio signal.* Seven. Seven. Three. Four.

All her exhilaration and enchantment vanished, replaced with irate panic. "Get the hell out!" she cried and pulled him to his feet. Chambers began stomping out the pattern. "Damn it," Henson growled and slapped his cheek.

The manic rhythm ended, and Chambers' helpless glance flew around the room before refocusing on her face. "Roberta?" He looked down at his naked chest and reddened with shame—like Adam, after the apple.

Without allowing him to say another word, Henson pushed Chambers out into the corridor and slammed the door. She rushed to the sink and splashed water on her face. Something was wrong.

Fifteen minutes later, Henson walked into the mess hall as promised. To her surprise, everyone else appeared to have arrived early, even Chambers. The postdoc and Bass stood on opposite sides, arguing. God knew where Meachem hid. Even odder, Captain Arthur was missing.

Bass, haggard and pale, had begun the rabble-rousing without her. "We need to send scouts out in every direction. If we stay here, we'll starve."

Chambers, now clear-eyed and fully clothed, yelled back, "It's too cold. Besides, it's a waste of gas to send out multiple snowmobiles on a wild goose chase. We should wait until we have some idea of where to go. When the sky clears, we can use the stars."

"The night is too small a window this time of year! We may not have time to wait for clear skies." The older man ran his fingers through his silver hair, causing the ordinarily well-coifed strands to stand on end. "People are beginning to show signs of cabin fever."

Henson studied the rest of the men. At least half of them held tools—tools that could double as weapons. Hammers. Screwdrivers. One postdoc clutched a red fire ax close to his chest. Most alarming to Henson were the firearms brandished by several of the crew.

They'd raided the makeshift armory. Nothing much, a few rifles and pistols, but enough to quicken Henson's pulse. Many of the people intently listened to Bass and Chambers' arguments, but not all. Several men looked around the room. She knew what played out in their heads. Counting. Calculating. Searching for 7734.

One thought bubbled up and then stuck in her head—now was the perfect time to rid herself of Bass. Why had she yearned for him to acknowledge her as his "peer" when she had outgrown this pathetic man long ago? A lone wrench sat on a nearby table. She imagined pounding Bass' brain to a pulp with exactly 7734 blows. Would any part of the skull remain after such a beating? More revolting was the worry she would tire and fall short of the magic number.

The volume of the crowd's bickering increased, ending Henson's violent fantasies.

"Running out of—"

"Drop the gun—"

"—do to Meachem and the captain?"

Everyone shouted each other down until it eventually all ran together in Henson's head.

"*... too cold why you pointing 7734 Captain Arthur! When did last made plain with stones 7734 no communication Henson 7734 last saw Meachem? Give me the rifle at the end is pit of 7734 NO HEAT nose blood just counted...*"

Henson could not chalk their antagonism up to fear or even ego. Minutes ago, she attempted to seduce her postdoc, and now giddy dreams of murder simmered in her brain. This "place" had allowed her dark desires to manifest when she both upstaged Bass and grew intimate with Chambers. Henson had traded her integrity for base pleasures, and now she forfeited both as each achievement twisted into perversion.

Henson shook her head and clapped her face. Had the entire ship gone mad? The smart thing was to even the playing field. The only other gun on the vessel lay in Captain Arthur's desk drawer. Better safe than sorry. No one noticed her slip out of the mess hall.

After a sprint down the corridor to the captain's quarters and a few knocks on his door, Henson turned the knob. "Captain?" She entered and flicked on the lights, driving away the darkness. Arthur reclined in the chair behind the desk with his head tipped over the backrest, obscuring his face. His hand gripped the revolver. Within a second, Henson noticed the crimson splatter covering the wall behind him and processed what had occurred. She doubled over. Why had the captain taken his own life? Did he blame himself for their predicament? Or was it—

Henson remained bent over for three more breaths before popping to attention. *No time for hysterics*. The captain had failed to go down with the ship, leaving the responsibility of saving the vessel to her. First, she needed to retrieve the weapon. While making sure to avoid looking at Arthur's head, she rounded the desk. She trembled as she tugged the revolver from his hand. The lifeless fingers fell away from the gunstock.

Henson had planned to pulverize the clenched fist with a paperweight or lamp. Instead, his limp hand felt surprisingly fresh, like he might awaken despite the hole in his head. With the gun in her right hand and the corpse's hand in her left, she paused. Henson flicked her wrist, and the weapon's cylinder popped open. Five bullets remained. *Good enough*. After squeezing his fingers goodbye, Henson shoved the gun into her pocket and released the captain. To Henson, only one course of action remained.

In minutes, she reached the external hatch. Frigid air blasted Henson as she stepped onto the deck. A gust ripped the door from her grip and slammed it into the wall. Inhuman voices called out above the howling wind—*7734, 7734, 7734*. Alone, she had no hope of exorcising the crew of the foul numeral. The remaining fuel would take one snowmobile farther than if they divvied it up. Farther still with a solo rider. No doubt, everyone on board the *Lady Dawn* would thank her when she returned.

Henson rushed to the snowmobiles and found several unsecured gasoline containers. As she lugged them to her chosen ride, questions ran through her head. *Who left the tanks on the deck? Shouldn't there be twice as many?*

After strapping each can to the vehicle, she hooked the hoist chains to the treads and sled. The hoist gears screeched louder than the wind as Henson lowered the snowmobile from the ship to the ice.

"Come on!" Henson glared at the hoist. The machine ground to a stop with the snowmobile still dangling ten feet above the ice.

A voice, decidedly human this time, called out. "Dr. Henson!"

To her left stood Meachem. He shivered without a coat. His hair was wet, matted down to his skull, and liquid dripped off his nose. The wind changed, so he now stood upwind from Henson. Fumes hit Henson's nose, and her breath caught a hitch as she noticed the gas canisters around his feet.

So, there's the rest of the gas.

"I'm so cold." Meachem flipped open his Zippo and lit the flame. His glassy eyes locked with Henson's. "Seven, seven, three—" Before he could finish his sentence, Meachem dropped the lighter. His body ignited, and he stood as a silent pillar of fire before the containers exploded.

The force knocked Henson off her feet. On her back, she looked up at the wan light fighting through the thick clouds. Shouts from the hatch jarred her to attention. The crew spilled from the opening like ants from a disturbed nest. Most of the wild-eyed men ran to the inferno, but Chambers remained in the hatchway.

"Roberta? What is going on?"

The reflection of the flames danced in his eyes. Henson remembered their days and nights together. They had achieved so much. For a moment, she thought to bring him with her.

Instead, Henson scaled the deck rail and jumped to the

snowmobile. The added weight sent the machine crashing to the ground. Chambers shouted at her, but the wind stole the words. Henson blew a goodbye kiss to the *Lady Dawn*.

Henson's gloved fingers fumbled with the keys. The snowmobile started seconds before bullets zipped past her, kicking up snow and ice. The entire crew now lined the deck's railing, shouting like savage apes. No regrets. She just hoped Chambers had not been one of the shooters.

***

A distant roar of wind tore Henson from her last memories aboard the *Lady Dawn*. A half-hour had passed since she had fled on the snowmobile. She gazed down at the broken fuel tanks and black pools of gasoline tarnishing the pristine ice. The fact she had no idea where she was heading now outweighed the fear of the dangers behind her. Surrounded by endless grayish-white, salvation felt farther away than on the stranded ship. The expedition had promised to solve a century-old mystery, but each occurrence since the *Buchanan's* discovery forced Henson to question her understanding of the world.

She shook off the dread and retrieved a compass from her pocket. A gleeful cry escaped Henson as she saw the compass needle pick a direction and stick with it. Due to luck or intuition, she had been heading south the entire time.

The moment of clarity proved short-lived as an awareness deep within her screamed one word.

Flee.

Without hesitation, Henson gunned the engine and aimed the machine south toward help. Henson felt as if something in her head played with a drawstring, dropping and raising a shroud over her mind. Her arms grew heavy on the handlebars, and her back ached. The thought of curling into a ball and closing her eyes seemed as crucial as fleeing until she noticed a distant black speck against the white world. With no alternatives, she turned the snowmobile in its direction. The spot grew more distinct until it solidified into a rectangle standing alone in the Arctic, like a stain remaining on a bleached shirt.

Thirty feet from the dark landmark, she saw the rectangle was a door standing in the frame of an igloo. How did something like this construct exist so far from civilization?

Henson cut the engine and dismounted the snowmobile. She scanned the horizon. Though she failed to see a single soul, Henson sensed countless eyes staring down on her. Terror gnawed at her, while her fight-or-flight response readied her for the unseen predator. Snow crunched beneath her boots as she rushed to the igloo's door.

The lack of weathering on both the smooth wood and polished metal struck her as strange. *Should I knock?* Henson brought her hand up to rap on the black mahogany but instead tried the golden doorknob. *No time for timidity.*

Henson turned the knob and entered. "Hello?" The structure was round but far more spacious than it appeared from the outside—by at least three times, she estimated.

Behind her, the door closed by itself, and she spun around. Henson clutched the revolver but kept it tucked in her pocket. The barren terrain had allowed her an unobstructed view in all directions. No one could have reached the igloo in so little time.

Must be the wind.

When her breathing slowed, she noticed it no longer produced steam. The igloo's heat and illumination emanated from a single-flame lantern. Its strange halation played off the icy walls. While studying the light, she relaxed. The Roberta Henson she knew was returning. As reason eclipsed superstition, her mind pounced on the immediate questions at hand. The lamp appeared vintage, from the *Buchanan's* time, but oddly had no discernable fuel source.

After poking and prodding the lantern from every angle, she pulled out her compass. The needle spun in a blur. "Of course." Resigned, she stuffed the useless instrument in her pocket.

Hours passed, slumber failed to arrive, and agitation gnawed at her like an elusive itch. Henson had hoped she would find help or a way to send a distress call from the structure. Heck, she would have settled for a map or any indication of her whereabouts. What now? Should she continue her journey southward or wait for the igloo's owner? The idea of returning to the *Lady Dawn* surfaced, but she would rather freeze than return to the ship's insanity. What she needed now was rest.

To calm her mind, Henson stopped debating her next move and began counting the ice blocks. About half the size of a brick, the identical rectangular tablets numbered too high to count. By her analytical nature, she divided the circular igloo into twelve equal parts like a clock. After tallying one sector, she could multiply by twelve to estimate the total number. Henson lost herself in the pleasure of counting. Anxiety melted away as she neared completion. With a smile on her face, she arrived at six hundred forty-four-and-a-half blocks. To Henson, something was soothing about that number. She pulled Chambers' old calculator from her pocket. Although she prided herself on her arithmetic skills, exhaustion had sapped her mind.

Henson removed her gloves to minimize the button mashing, and on the third try, she had her answer.

7734 blocks.

It can't be. Henson dashed the calculator against the wall. *I left that number on the sh—* Without missing a beat, something knocked on the door like it heard the calculator hit the ground. *Was it watching her?*

Knock.

Did it want shelter, or did it want *her*?

Knock. Knock. Knock.

Her legs turned to jelly as the outsider lost its patience and pounded on the door.

KNOCK! KNOCK! KNOCK!

The terror reminded her of her teen years when she was home alone, and an unknown stranger banged at the front door.

Then the igloo began shaking as a tremendous force struck the walls. Whatever had pounded on the door now threatened to demolish the structure. The walls shook, and ice dropped from the ceiling, shattering on the floor like glass. Henson crouched in the igloo's center and prayed. Blinding white powder churned around the igloo before the assault subsided. Deceitful silence filled the air as the swirling snow settled around her.

Pain shocked her from the fetal position. Henson looked down in horror at a frozen shard, now protruding from her thigh. She clenched her teeth and pulled it free. Shaking, she tossed the icicle away and pressed on the wound with her gloves.

The doorknob rattled like it would break off. Experiences of long-ago dread filled Henson, not from her teen years this time, but as a child in bed awaiting the boogeyman. Should she cry or scream?

Wide-eyed, she rubbed the nape of her neck but then stopped. One fact differentiated her current situation and her terrifying childhood memories. *She was armed.* Henson pulled the gun from her pocket and aimed it at the door. She shut her eyes and squeezed the trigger.

Click.

Henson opened her eyes and confirmed five bullets remained in the cylinder. She aimed again.

Click. Click. Click. Click. Click.

The gun fell from her grip, and she brought her hands to her mouth to stifle a scream. The noise behind the door stopped, causing her to stiffen in place.

The doorknob then began to turn.

Henson stumbled and dove to the door. She let out a broken shriek and grasped the knob with both hands. It continued spinning under supernatural strength, and the door cracked open.

Frigid wind and snow rushed into the warm interior, stinging her like a swarm of demonic wasps. For a moment, the lamp's flame roared in an infernal fire before it died down, and the bright interior darkened. Oneiric shadows of nonexistent beasts danced across the empty room's shiny walls, taunting her.

What was on the other side of the door?

It must be a bear. Yes, a polar bear. I didn't see it because of the white camouflage. What else could it be up here in no-man's-land? What's the worst it could be?

As if offering her an answer, the number 7734 flashed in her head. Should she quit the pointless battle and just look? Seeing her opponent would mean it was of this world and not her nightmares.

A number can't open a door.

Henson winced as her quivering injured leg splashed blood around her feet. Every muscle tensed until her bones felt ready to break. Still, she slid across the ground as the door pushed open inch by inch.

Please be a bear. An animal would only take Henson's life, not her soul.

Scanning the room for another weapon, she caught sight of her spilled blood. The splatters formed into a single vermilion stream and coursed to the calculator like iron filings to a magnet. Now, viewed upside-down, the device gave Henson its actual answer in letters, not numbers. She remembered wasting time with this trick in junior high math. Trapped in the ship or trapped in the igloo—Hawaii was a million miles away.

When turned on its head, the digits 7734 revealed her location—*hELL.*

* * *

AISLE THREE

BY ROSIE O'CARROLL

There was an air to aisle three that always gave me the creeps. The section was several degrees colder compared to the rest of the store, but that was hardly unusual as it housed all the meat. I suspect it stemmed from the story Biker Pete used to tell me about his cousin, Lenny. Biker Pete was always recounting some fantastic tale, usually when he'd moved on to Scotch, but aisle three was one of his favorites.

In the early hours of the morning, Lenny was patrolling the store when he happened to look down the meat aisle. Standing at the far end, he saw a man dressed in black overalls. The figure acknowledged him with an odd little smile and raising his right hand, slowly beckoned to Lenny to come closer. Lenny panicked and fled through the store, but by the time he reached the exit, the man had vanished.

During all my years at Vinten's, I'd never come across, what Lenny had later named as the "Supermarket Spook." And I reminded myself Lenny was a drunk, which was why Management fired him and I got his job. But Pete's story stayed with me, and I'd catch myself hesitating as I walked past aisle three on my hourly sweep of the store.

I guess ten years was a long time in any job. Mom used to say, "Oh Leo, why do you keep slaving away in that depressing old store? You're an intelligent boy!" I guess she had a point. I was all set for university, but after Dad died, it didn't seem right to head off and leave Mom on her own. Besides, the work suited me, and Security was a step up from my Saturday job manning the tills. Working nights kept me out of Mom's way, and once the shelf fillers had gone home, it was just me and the CCTV. I read my books and made sure the fridges stayed on. No burglar ever blew off the doors, at least not on my watch. It was as silent as the grave, aside from the odd rodent, skittering past and looking for treats.

Eventually, though, I had to admit the role was losing its novelty, which was why I ended up stealing stuff. Age-wise, my big "30" was looming, and all my friends were settling down or driving BMWs. I drove the second-hand Volvo my Dad bought me for my 18th birthday, still sporting its original beaded seat covers. One day, I checked the state of my overdraft and decided the minimum wage was a little ungenerous. My job needed a few perks—which would necessitate skills not usually detailed on one's curriculum vitae. Thinking back now, I had a suspicion my thieving may have stirred something up. It began with the extra strong mints. I sauntered past the row of shelves by the cash registers and slipped the tiny packet into my pocket. Acting all innocent, I strolled back to my office and rewound the CCTV to see if I could spot myself stealing. The screen view divided to display multiple cameras at once, and it took only minutes to search for any incriminating footage. Who knew I'd be a natural? Mission accomplished.

I was careful not to take any items the other staff were likely to notice—like spirits with a security tag or any of those ridiculously priced razors. At least at the start. Mints were upgraded to Snickers bars and soon progressed to a whole pack of cookies. Small things, but it was amazing how much they cheered up the night shift. Like I said, perks.

A few weeks into my forays into felony, I noticed the atmosphere in the supermarket had deteriorated. It was never a warm and cozy place, but apart from aisle three, I'd found it sterile and functional. But now it adopted a darker edge as if altered in a way I couldn't explain. As I walked past the rows of vegetables and pasta, the back of my neck and shoulders prickled. It was as if a primeval part of my brain had lit up, sensing someone or something was watching me. My rational mind knew the store was empty, so I attributed it to the beginnings of a guilty conscience. I lay off pilfering for a few days, shrugging it off as a fit of the paranoids, but as soon as I resumed, so did the feeling I was no longer alone.

The change in atmosphere piqued my curiosity about the history of the store, so I took a day off and headed to the local records office. I found it as cluttered and as fusty as my last visit when I studied the archives for A-Level History. The newspaper catalogue seemed an excellent place to start. Perhaps I'd read of a shelf filler squashed by an avalanche of cans, or a customer croaking at the sight of their grocery bill. My only clue to a timeframe was 1953, the date etched by the architect above the store entrance. But with little else to go on, I wished I'd brought a flask.

I was about to give up when a headline caught my eye. The article described the court proceedings of a brutal murder, and I did a double-take when I saw the photo of the location of the crime. The picture showed the outside of a factory, which, thirty years later, changed into a supermarket—the same supermarket where I worked.

The accused was a foreman called John Norris, who, upon discovering a workman stealing supplies from the factory, flew into a rage and killed the unfortunate thief with an axe. Norris attempted to dispose of the body by chopping it up into pieces and concealing the remains in different locations around the town. This must be my spook! The spirit of the victim, wandering the store where he met his vicious and untimely demise—now with nothing better to do except watch me from the shadows. Maybe Lenny wasn't as crazy after all. I returned to work, and although the place seemed as dour as ever, I shrugged it off as echoes from the past.

The actual incident, hallucination—name it as you wish, happened on a cold night in March. Spring was still hiding from a threat of late snow, and Easter was due early. I'd gotten my heart set on a nice half-leg of lamb—perfect for weaving my culinary magic with garlic and rosemary and a side of mint sauce. I knew this heist would be hard to pull off. Lamb joints are odd-shaped and bulkier than cookies, but this would add to the excitement. Even though I could erase the footage, I liked to challenge myself to shoplift discreetly.

When the shelf-fillers departed, I flicked off the main lights to maximize profit as the owners instructed. The glow emanating from the dairy section and the fridges in aisle three gave enough light to see by, but I wasn't a fan of the darkness. When I started my patrols, I'd switch everything on, but this time I noticed the lights flicker and flash, fading and brightening in rapid succession before several went out completely. The fridges didn't appear to be affected, so I could wait to call the electrician in the morning. I had enough light to see by, but the missing bulbs made the store appear gloomier than ever. The fridges buzzed softly, like a swarm of invisible insects. It was too early for the dawn chorus or the comforting hum of early morning traffic. The only word I could think of to describe it was... *isolated*. I finished my tour in double-quick time and returned to my office to wait.

I planned my next patrol at 4 am. I wanted to take the lamb near the end of my shift to make sure the meat wouldn't be out of the fridge for too long. I marked the page I'd gotten to in my thriller, grabbed my phone in case the electricity failed altogether and pulled on my company fleece, leaving it half unzipped. I'd devised the crime well in advance. I'd pretend to bend down to do up my shoelace, and with one hand, I'd slip the joint in the side of my jacket. I'd then make my way back to my office. Job done.

As I walked into the store, the gloomy sensation returned, enveloping me like a heavy woollen blanket. I tried to put the impression behind me and carried on to aisle three, wishing the newspaper story hadn't chosen that moment to pop back into my mind.

I exhaled loudly. The aisle was empty. The legs of lamb were kept halfway along, and I'd already earmarked the perfect joint, amounting to a saving of £17.00. I walked to the side of the fridge and went through the motions of tying my shoelaces. As I bent down, I whipped the joint into my jacket and pulled up the zip. It had worked like a dream—or so I believed until I stood up and saw movement at the end of the aisle. A flash of black registered in the corner of my eye. Uncertain of what I had seen, I walked over to the end of the aisle and looked down toward the end of the store. I held my breath, listening for footsteps. Had someone finally gotten the guts to try and break in?

I waited for a few minutes and satisfied I couldn't hear anything; I made a quick tour of the store to make sure there was no other lamb thief looking to get lucky. The only living soul I spotted was a rat that ran past at high speed and scuttled down a hole in a far corner. I'd have to ask the manager to restock the poison.

With no logical explanation for the dark shadow, I blamed it on tiredness. It had been a long night, and I forced all thoughts of shadowy figures from my mind. There was no way I was listening to Biker Pete again.

Shutting the door of the store and locking it behind me, I went back to the office. I could feel the coldness of the meat burrowing into my stomach and couldn't wait to remove the joint from my jacket. I shoved the lamb in a plastic carrier bag on my desk, ready to take with me when I left. Fancy spooking myself for the sake of a roast dinner.

Now, to check and rate my performance. I sat down at the computer and rewound the CCTV footage, confident I would ace it like a pro. I watched myself walk through the supermarket, and then I cried out and clicked on the pause button. *What the hell was that?* It looked like I was being followed through the store by a swirling black mist. I leant forward, bringing my face so close to the screen I was almost kissing the monitor. I hit play again and sure enough saw a mass of darkness creeping behind me, dispersing into the air when I reached aisle three.

I stopped and played the footage again. There must be a fault somewhere, or interference from a nearby drug dealer's phone. The mist was still visible. I wound the video on a few more seconds. I could see myself bending down, but this time there was no mistaking it—I wasn't alone. The mist remained, but now it had coalesced into a solid shape. A man-like shape. Pain stung the back of my eyes as I stared transfixed at the screen. The black form drifted forward until it—no he—was standing right next to me. I saw myself go through the motions of the shoe-tying and slipping the joint into my jacket, entirely oblivious to the fact he was there. As I continued to watch, I realized my attempt at hiding the lamb was more visible than I'd hoped, and I started to panic. The veins in my temples began to pound, both from fear of being caught and terror at the sight of the unexplained shape. Watching me was one thing, but I had no desire to make the victim's acquaintance.

I fumbled with the keyboard, and after two abortive attempts, I finally managed to erase the footage. I slumped back in the chair, inhaling and exhaling in short sharp gulps, and noticed the metallic taste of blood. I winced as I ran my finger over my bottom lip. I must have bitten down hard without realizing. I was relieved the footage had gone. I had no wish to see it again.

I wasn't given long to relax. The clang of metal as something slammed against the door that led back into the supermarket sent me springing from my chair. I turned back to look at the CCTV screens. The supermarket appeared empty, but the noise reverberated again as if a can of beans had flown off the shelf and struck the side of an aisle. Yet the door was nowhere near the tinned goods. I waited for the strike of metal to repeat, but the store fell silent. My heart pounded as I waited for the cameras to display a clear view of aisle three. When they did so, I groaned. No terrifying figure or mist danced across the screen. The only thing out of place was a small object lying on the floor in the middle of the aisle.

Fumbling around the pockets of my fleece, I swore again. Yep, my mobile was missing. Maybe it had fallen out while I'd crouched down or dropped when I'd slipped the lamb into my jacket. Either way, I couldn't avoid going back into the supermarket to retrieve it. I just hoped my phone wasn't the thing I'd heard hurled against the door before something transported it over to aisle three.

I took a deep breath and tried to convince myself my eyes were tired, and ghosts only existed in stories. I opened the door to the shop, expecting a spook to jump out at me the second I stepped over the threshold. Instead, a foul smell hit me in the face, and I almost retched.

Putrid meat. It smelt like the pack of mince that had fallen out of my shopping bag on a hot summer's day and lay rotting in my car for a week.

I pinched my nose with one hand and covered my mouth with the other to try and avoid being sick. *Had the refrigerators failed when the lights went out?* If the food started spoiling, I'd be in big trouble. Forgetting all about ghosts, I ran over to aisle three and picked up my phone from the floor. The smell was becoming overpowering, but the air around the fridges still had a chill about it. I looked down the side of the units trying to locate the thermometer, and that's when I happened to glance down at the meat. In the time between stealing the lamb and returning to pick up the phone, the contents of the aisle had changed. The first thing I noticed was the sausages. Visible through the plastic shrink wrap, I could see their color and shape were no longer the uniform pink and beige oblongs I remembered. Instead, they were a row of bloodied human fingers whose broken nail tips were starting to break through the packaging. I could make out the ridges of knuckles and saw the hint of stumps disappearing into the edge of the polystyrene packaging. In the section beside them, the rows of bland trussed chickens had transmogrified into the heads of men, women, and children, whose dead eyes peered upwards to the ceiling, forever unblinking. Next to the heads were trays of tiny hands and ears, as if waiting to be purchased for ungodly cannibal casseroles. And opposite the pork and lamb joints now resembled severed body parts. As I stared open-mouthed, I heard a low rumbling laugh emanating from the end of aisle three.

I didn't wait to greet the dark figure, which I knew would be standing waiting to greet me. I ran back to my office and made it to my desk as nausea overwhelmed me. I managed to grab hold of the wastepaper basket before reacquainting myself with the contents of my dinner.

The sickness made me dizzy, but I wasn't going to wait around to feel better. I grabbed the plastic carrier bag from the table, ran out of the door at the back and locked up. I threw the bag in the front seat of the Volvo and drove off. Everything in that supermarket could rot for all I cared. I was done with that job. I quit.

The first rays of light were beginning to appear over the horizon as I headed home. As I focused on the road in front of me, my breathing slowed down, and my rational mind returned. The dismemberment of the victim must have sunk into my brain and was now wreaking havoc with my subconscious. Did I seriously think that within the space of ten minutes, aisle three had been emptied and restocked with the contents of a serial killer's store cupboard? Had I eaten something weird or had a flashback from a teenage trip? I stopped my car at the traffic lights, relieved to think that in 20 minutes, I'd be home in bed. The road in front and behind was deserted. I looked out to the field to my left, abundant with winter wheat swaying in a silent breeze. The bag with the lamb sat on the front seat next to me, and as I waited for a green light, I noticed a rustling sound. I glanced down, just as the middle of the bag shifted on the seat. Then the whole bag inched a little way forward and rustled again as if something was alive within it. I yanked on the handbrake, threw off my seatbelt and pushed the passenger door open. I flung the bag as hard as I could out onto the side of the road, and after slamming the door shut and returning to my seat, I stamped on the accelerator. As the car sped away, the tires screeching like a demon, I had a horrible compulsion to peer in my rear-view mirror. As I did so, I saw the outline of a man standing in the empty road behind me. I dared not look back until I had reached the safety of home.

I gave up being a security guard and vowed never to return to Vinten's. If the victim was trying to warn me to give up thieving, he'd certainly done the trick. I sold my car, got a student loan, and started a history degree at my local college. Mom was right: it was time I did something with my life. I never saw the dark figure again, but he did make a reappearance in my life a few weeks later, in a way I would never have expected.

I was sitting in the Dog and Fox when in walked Biker Pete.

Remembering him as a connoisseur of cheap cider, I bought him a pint, and we were soon standing at the bar gossiping like old mates. Eventually, I plucked up the courage to tell him my story, (although I left out the stealing and the morphing of the meat).

"But there is one thing I don't understand," I said. "Why, did I hear the victim laughing even though he'd suffered such a terrible fate?"

Biker Pete took a draught of his pint and shook his head. "I thought you knew, Leo. It isn't the victim who is haunting aisle three. It's the foreman who couldn't stand thieves."

I gripped hold of the bar, steadying myself as the realization of who had been watching me slowly sunk in. But it was Pete's next tale that sent a chill through me like a crack of a whip.

"I'm not surprised the store is haunted. The more accounts of the murder I read, the more gruesome the details become—especially the scattergun approach to dumping the body. A week after the murder, a farmer spotted a small bag lying in the corner of his field, and as he approached it, the bag appeared to be moving. When he pulled the bag open, he discovered the rotting remains of a human foot, severed at the ankle and writhing with maggots."

* * *

Pumpkin Patch

By C. B. Channell

Bobby Burkitt crept around the side of the house, careful to remain below the windowsills. It was *the* house. Every town had one—an old, not-quite-decrepit house occupied by an elderly widower. The old man. The house, the old man.

And his pumpkin patch.

And at Halloween season, these things grew in importance exponentially.

Bobby was on the side of the house and clearly visible to anyone, say, across the street who might look out of a second story or attic window in his direction. Or to the next-door neighbors on that side, if they leaned over the weakened fence and pushed aside tree branches. He stood up quickly, peering carefully.

Nope, he was hidden pretty well. The concern wasn't those of others; it was the old man. Of course.

Not that Bobby could explain exactly *why* he was so threatening, beyond the obvious trespassing issue. But everyone in every town knew—whoever the old person was in the old, decaying house was dangerous in some very mysterious way.

Bobby put his weight on his left knee, his other leg twisted at a right angle and his right hand pressed against the flaking siding. He crept along, knee, foot, knee, foot, careful to move twigs and anything else out of the way that might make noise. He moved slowly but was proud of his stealth. Watching his family's cat for years had finally paid off, no matter what his older brother and his friends said.

The thought of them made him bristle and he paused, afraid of making noise. It was because of them that he was here. Although it seemed like a solid idea at first, before the details were worked out, the reality of being here—under the old man's window, with dusk about to fall, and him trying to work his way to the back yard. *Could the old man be in the back yard?* he thought with a sudden chill. Now, it seemed, well, not such a solid idea.

It was a week before Halloween. It was time for the pumpkin; it was family tradition. If he didn't come home with one then the family would just drive to the big farm just outside town and buy one there. Like they did every year. Like they expected to do that night.

Except he wasn't there, and they wouldn't leave without him. But he had to steal one of the old man's pumpkins and get it home before they totally freaked out and started the whole town searching for him.

One stupid dare. But even though the shivers grew as the shadows lengthened and the sky turned indigo, he wasn't going to give up. He was determined to show his brother and his brother's friends once and for all that he could bring home the family Halloween pumpkin. He would be a hero.

And surely, the old man would never know the difference. His lot was huge and his pumpkin patch, while not a farm, was still big. Really big. What was one pumpkin?

It was the edge of darkness when he finally managed to enter the backyard garden. By now, he was on his belly, scooting along. He glanced repeatedly over his shoulder toward the back door to make sure no one was there; his luck held. He crept between tomato plants and bean poles. The garden was messy but organized, and it wasn't hard to get to the back part of the lot where melons and squash, including the pumpkins, grew.

The pumpkins were furthest back, and distantly, he thought it would have been easier to find a way to enter the yard from the back. There would have been a little chance of being seen, but the edge of the yard abutted a ravine that was filled with thorny bushes and weedy, prickly plants. The truth was, he didn't know how deep that ravine went underneath the plants, and he didn't want to get trapped and find out bad news the hard way.

Scraping along, he was now making some noise. From all the adventure comics he'd read, he knew that the pounding he was hearing was his own heart and that no one else could hear it, and that the incredibly loud crackling of vegetation beneath him was more of a whisper on the breeze than the sound of an elephant tromping through the jungle. He forced himself to keep his sense of reality.

He was just there for a pumpkin.

A really, really good pumpkin.

Six years later (or so it seemed), he reached the pumpkin patch. It was dark now, though the sky wasn't entirely black yet. There were still patches of dark indigo and a half-moon shone brightly upon him. Luckily, where he was, the streetlights were too far away to drown the moonlight on one hand and expose him on the other. He realized he had to choose his pumpkin based on size and feel; he could only hope the color would be perfect. So, he set about his task.

After about ten minutes, he grew frustrated. It seemed that, even though he carefully scoped out the shapes, when he reached for them, they weren't there. Well, they were there, but they were just out of reach. The darkness continued to deepen. Soon enough, the light shifted. Bobby glanced up and realized the moon was high in the inky blackness. He'd been in the patch itself for at least half an hour. His family was definitely looking for him, or about to. Unless his brother had owned up, and Bobby sincerely doubted that that would ever happen.

He snorted once in determination and forged ahead, no longer worried about being heard, and wrapped his arms around the nearest big pumpkin.

"Yaaah!" he shouted, jumping back. He lifted his hand and stared at it, stunned. Black, sticky stuff covered his palm where he'd grasped the pumpkin. He'd cut himself. With a shock, he realized how loudly he'd shouted, and his head whipped around. He hoped no one had heard him, or if they had, didn't know what the sound was and ignored him.

His breathing grew louder and more ragged as he scanned the terrain behind him. When he finally decided that he was safe, he drew in a deep breath of relief and turned back to his task.

And met the pumpkin's teeth.

***

Twenty Years Later

Kevin Burkitt stepped on to the front porch. The screen door slammed behind him. He absently took a sip from his coffee cup.

Since he'd grown up, the town both changed and didn't. Still the same old Victorian monstrosities with huge porches like the one he stood on. Still the same old little stores and businesses, but fewer of course, since the big boxes moved in an hour away near the next town. Still the same neighbors, or at least the same families of those neighbors. Still. Still.

He'd managed to get away after high school, but his mother became ill and his father began slowly losing his mind. His wife was from elsewhere and not keen on returning to his family home, but they had no other good options. At least his daughter was still just past toddler age. With any luck, this detour in their lives wouldn't last long, and they could move back to somewhere normal before she was old enough to remember clearly.

He shook his head, berating himself for such thoughts. It wasn't right to wish your parents dead, after all.

But I don't wish them dead, he told himself, starting up the same argument with himself he'd had a thousand times. I just want them living somewhere with assistance. Someone *else's* assistance.

But that wasn't going to happen, at least not now, and he had to deal with the reality in front of him. And that reality was Halloween.

Not just any Halloween. The twentieth-anniversary Halloween.

The Halloween where Bobby—probably Bob or Robert by now—would have been twenty-seven, maybe even a college degree, maybe even a family, maybe still living in this backward, superstitious old town.

What if, what if. Well, Bobby was gone. Had been gone twenty years. No one knew where or how. The last they knew he'd gone off on a dare into old man Harlow's pumpkin patch. Well, maybe. He'd gone off into Harlow's property, but whether he'd made it back from the pumpkin patch, no one ever knew. He simply didn't come back.

The memories of that had come quickly when he let himself open the floodgates. At first, Kevin and Rick thought Bobby was playing with them, to get them back at them for their mean dare, but as it grew later and Kevin's mom became more and more worried, they decided to take matters into their own hands. If they could get to Bobby first and convince him not to tattle, there would be little trouble. Maybe they'd all get sent to bed without supper and life would go on. Kevin would pay Bobby back with excess Halloween candy. Everything would be fine. But old man Harlow, being what he was, refused to let Kevin and his best friend Rick go back and search for Bobby. He said he'd do it himself.

But after Harlow had been gone for nearly twenty minutes, Kevin grew restless. He told Rick to stay in front of the old house in case someone came by and then ran to the backyard to find the old man and his brother. The old man was in the pumpkin patch. He had a hoe.

Kevin approached him nervously. Was he seriously gardening at night, with Bobby missing? As he drew nearer to the strange, scary Harlow, he began to hope that Bobby had run home. Even if he had tattled it would have been better than this creeping fear. Kevin continued to drag along as quietly as he could until he passed the main vegetable garden and made it to the pumpkin patch.

He moved toward Harlow who then turned and grinned a horrible, toothy, jack o' lantern grin at him, with hoe in one hand. Kevin glanced down and saw the pumpkin that Harlow was cultivating. The light from Harlow's flashlight cast a shadow on the ground where the pumpkin was. For the briefest second, Kevin thought the pumpkin looked like his little brother's face contorted into a scream. He opened his mouth to say something, but Harlow wheeled on him, brandishing the hoe threateningly.

"Get out! I told you you couldn't come back here! Your brat brother isn't here, but he messed up my patch good and now I have to fix it and I still haven't had my dinner! Shoo! Shoo!" He raised the hoe and waved it at Kevin who turned and fled as fast as he could.

Of course, they called the police. And of course, the police searched Harlow's property. But there was no sign of Bobby. The weeks that followed were a nightmare circus, but in the end, Bobby was gone. Simply gone.

At first, people thought he must have been kidnapped, but there was no ransom demand. The official explanation, eventually, was that the boy had run away. He went into the missing children's register and that was that. Not case closed, but case no longer pursued. Kevin's family became the family that lost their little boy on Halloween, pitied and talked about in hushed tones.

Even after all those years.

He went to take another sip of coffee, but it was ice cold. He tossed what little was left into the untrimmed hedges in front of the porch. He was about to turn and go back in when he saw movement down the street. He leaned over the steps and saw someone just turn around and slip away. Someone had been standing there staring at him. He tried to get a closer look, but whoever it was moved away too quickly.

He shook his head. Halloween was the next day. He was stuck in that awful town with the memories of Bobby and the aftermath, his own life in disarray.

The early coolness wore off, and the town came slowly to life. Early to rise was a moral imperative in nowheresville, but early to get moving also wasn't as much.

And why would it? This stupid little town is dying, he thought. It was overwhelmingly populated with people his parents' age or older.

They were dying off, and they were determined not to leave.

Why not? He looked around, seeing the town through his wife's eyes. It wasn't quaint; it didn't have sweet little antique shops and diners and candy stores. It was dilapidated, a relic. The people here weren't happy, but they were stubborn. His mother remained only because she still thought Bobby might come home. He squeezed his eyes shut for a moment, breathed in deeply, then opened them again.

In the same place a few minutes ago, someone stood staring at him. This time, he didn't move. And Kevin could have sworn it was old man Harlow.

***

"Oh yeah, old man Harlow. Lives a couple blocks over. Strange fellow, think there was something..." said his father, trailing off as he was wont to do anymore. "Clara, wasn't there something, some scandal a few years back?" he frowned, furrowing his brow, trying desperately to remember. Kevin couldn't bear it.

"Old man Harlow can't still be alive," he sighed.

"Kevin," said his mother warningly.

"Oh, yeah, he's alive. Think I just saw him at the garden store. He was getting... something for... he grows all that stuff." His father frowned again.

"Vegetables," said his mother helpfully. "And pumpkins."

"Right!" said his father, his eyes lighting up. "That pumpkin patch! But he never let anyone have a pumpkin at Halloween. Always got to go out of town for pumpkins." He rubbed his chin and took a sip out of his empty coffee cup. He didn't seem to notice. "So, we're gonna have to get a pumpkin. It's Halloween tomorrow, after all." He smiled at Kevin who only half-heartedly smiled back. "It's good you're here this year," he continued. "Bobby's missed you."

"Harvey!" snapped Clara.

Kevin looked sharply at his mother then turned his attention back to his father. His features softened and he looked sad, almost defeated. "Dad. Bobby's gone. He's not here."

"Of course not," said his father, chuckling. "But he'll be by tomorrow, during trick-or-treats. Every year. Harlow's taken good care of him. He said so."

"All right, Harvey," said Kevin's mother. "You've finished your coffee. Time for a lie down." She gathered him together and got him into the bedroom.

Later, while his father was napping, Kevin joined his mother in the living room. She was sipping a cup of tea and staring at the television. It was off.

"Mom," he said, sitting beside her on the couch.

"I don't want to hear it, Kevin," she said, shaking her head.

"I don't care," he replied. He was angry; he'd fought bitterly with his wife last night. He glanced out the window, toward the spot across the street where he thought he'd seen old man Harlow. No one was there. The town was quiet.

Quiet as the grave, he thought. He tried to remember what it was like when he and Bobby were little. Wasn't there always something going on, right before Halloween? Deciding on costumes? What to trick if they didn't get their treats? What candies they were willing to trade, what they wanted to get? How to avoid razor blades in fruit? In his mind, that was Halloween *before*. There was no Halloween *after*.

"Mom," he pressed. "You can't keep taking care of dad. He's going to wander off..."

"Where? So, he wanders off. There's nowhere to go in this town. Besides, everyone knows him. Knows us."

"Yeah. Knows you're the people who won't let go of the past! Knows the only reason you stay in this falling down house," he waved his arms to indicate the peeling, sagging monstrosity his childhood home had become, "is because you think your seven-year-old is coming home any day now. He's not. Just because dad sees him... Mom, he's gone. Dad's mind isn't... strong. He's imagining this."

She turned to him, eyes blazing. "I know he's not seven. But something happened, and he's been trying to get back to us, every year. And he will. I know it. I hear his voice at night, especially now."

Kevin frowned. "What do you mean, especially now?"

She turned away and sipped her tea.

"Mom!"

"He's here. We can't leave. Not at Halloween."

He tried a little longer to make her see reason, see that dad had to be in a place with professionals; she wasn't qualified to care for him. Period.

"Daddy!" Alana ran into the room and tumbled into his legs.

"Hi, gidget." He scooped her into his lap.

"Can we go trick or treating tomorrow? Here?" She pointed out the window. The room went silent. Even the dust motes seemed to freeze in place.

"I don't know," he said slowly. "You don't even have a costume."

"Mommy's going to make me one. Grandma's going to help. Then she'll take me 'round. She said so!"

Kevin eyed his mother angrily, but she refused to look at him.

"I don't know if that's such a good idea," he repeated.

"Mommy said it was okay."

He grimaced. *That's one way to convince me to leave here, Marcy*, he thought. Not that he needed much convincing. But he did need to convince his mother. He wished he could rush that, but this would be difficult. And he didn't want to do it alone, which was why his family was with him.

If only his wife were truly *with* him.

"Is Mommy going with you?"

Alana nodded emphatically.

"Oh, let her go. Honestly, your father isn't going to get into any trouble. Not here, not in this town. Not..."

"Not on Halloween? 'Cause nothing ever happens here?" he retorted. He was angry. Angry with his father for getting sick, angry with his mother for avoiding reality, angry with Bobby for disappearing. With Harlow for being Harlow and having a pumpkin patch, with Marcy, his wife, with everyone, with himself for daring his brother on that Halloween so long ago. Mostly for that.

"Dad needs professional help. You can't even keep this house up," he repeated for what felt like the thousandth time in a low voice.

She slammed her cup down on the coffee table. "Fine, Kevin, if it will make you go away."

Alana curled up a little tighter in her father's lap, staring at her grandmother. Grandma relented, relaxed a bit and reached for her granddaughter's hand.

"Sorry, pigeon," she said.

"Gidget," corrected Kevin.

It registered for a moment. "After my favorite TV show. When I was about Bobby's age," she said. She looked up at Kevin, tears in her eyes. "You remembered."

"She found the show on one of those oldies stations," he said, brushing her off. He didn't want to get sentimental, not just now. He had to make phone calls quickly before his mother changed her mind. He'd laid the groundwork, but he had to put things in motion, make it near impossible for his mother to reverse direction. Her future he'd deal with after dad was safe.

Alana squirmed. He hugged her then set her down, her feet running practically before she hit the floor.

One more thing before that, he thought, *find Marcy*. Put the trick-or-treat ideas right out of her head. He would promise to do some kind of Halloween celebration of their own, after. At home. In the city, where he didn't let his daughter trick-or-treat, and they never got a pumpkin.

***

Halloween

It's not right, thought Kevin as he stared out the kitchen window, sipping coffee. The day was sunny and mild. The foliage was bright fall. It didn't look like any Halloween he remembered.

How can the town look so different today? he wondered. All week it had been dismal; every Halloween in his memory was dim and rainy. But for some reason, it looked like a fresh, fall-harvest town today. He shook his head and then stopped.

Someone was moving, just beyond the back fence. He leaned into the window, trying to get a better look. The figure was furtive, but definitely looking at his house.

Old man Harlow, he thought, recognizing the shirt from yesterday. He knew it couldn't be, but he peered closer, debated whether or not to go outside and chase the old creep away.

Just then the old man leaned over the fence and met Kevin's eyes, even from that distance, even through the trees. He grinned. Kevin started and dropped his coffee cup on the counter, spilling.

He looked like Bobby. Bobby's face on the old man, but wrinkled. And orange. That jack o' lantern face from twenty years before but with his baby brother's features. He blinked and the figure was gone, shuffling down the alley. All Kevin could see then was the back of the dirty old shirt.

"This place makes me lose my mind," he muttered. He put the coffee cup in the sink and went into the living room.

Dad was sitting in his chair staring at the blank television. He could hear feminine murmurs and giggles from down the hall. He followed the sound.

Mom and Marcy were helping Alana put together a costume. There wasn't much to work with, but Alana was going through her grandmother's old jewelry.

"Daddy!" she cried exultantly. "I'm going to be the old Comtessa!" she stood up, draped in a worn silk jacket and tons of chunky necklaces and bracelets.

"So, you're really going to do this?" he asked.

Marcy sighed. "She wants to, and we're stuck here anyway," she said, not looking up. Clara shot her a look, but she ignored it. Kevin turned and just kept himself from storming out of the room.

Later, after they'd had a late breakfast, Marcy bundled Alana up despite the girl's protests and prepared to leave.

"Don't go to Harlow's house," said Kevin in a dead voice. He sat on the couch beside his father's chair.

"I don't even know where that is," said Marcy in her sharp way.

"I bet Uncle Bobby knows," said Alana.

They all stared at her. "You don't have an Uncle Bobby," said Kevin carefully.

"Yes, I do!" she said excitedly. "He's here! Not here, like in the house, I mean, but here, you know, around!"

"Alana..." he began.

"Yes, you're right dear," said Clara. "Uncle Bobby is around."

Really? he thought. He stared at his daughter and felt a wave of love, fear, and exhaustion plunge through him. He opened his mouth, but before he could speak, his father said, "You look mighty pretty" to Alana. She preened.

"Thank you, Grandpa. I'll bring you some candy!"

"Does anyone still give out candy around here?" Kevin asked his mother. "I mean, are there any children left in this town?"

His mother pursed her lips and glared at him. "Not as many as there used to be, but they're here. People will give out candy."

"Where's your candy, then?" he asked.

She glanced away.

"Fine. I'll go buy some candy," he said, grabbing his jacket. He couldn't stand being there anymore. He'd come here to help, if not to fix things, but at least to make them better. He was thwarted at every step, so why not just give in?

"Harlow's house is on Begonia Street. Just stay off that street completely," he said to his wife as he slammed the screen door behind him.

He got in the car before he realized he'd left his keys in the house. He couldn't bear to go back inside just yet, so he decided to walk to downtown. He'd wanted to go to the big box store and grab the candy and a few things he thought his father might like, but that was out of the question now. Whatever was still open in this dying place was where he was going.

At least the weather's cooperating, he thought.

Most of the stores on the main drag were closed, but there was the tiny pharmacy in the middle of the block. All they had left was some old hard candy that he suspected could have been there since Bobby disappeared. He bought a bag, stepped out, and saw the old tavern across the street.

What the hell.

Hours later he was feeling comfortably drunk. He debated having another drink, but thought better of it. He left a generous tip, grabbed his bag of hideous old candy and left.

Still unwilling to go home and face the family that clearly didn't want him around, he wandered. His drunk-fogged mind kept trying to focus, memories of his childhood mixing with thoughts of his daughter, his parents, his marriage (what there was of it), and Harlow.

Harlow.

How was he still alive? How was he still here? Was that even him? Why did he look like Bobby?

He shook his head. He hadn't eaten anything, and the combination of coffee and beer left him lightheaded. He stared at his feet as he walked.

Left foot. Right foot. His brain finally grew numb. He focused on his feet as he walked, one two, one two. He blinked, then stumbled over a broken piece of sidewalk.

He stopped, drew a deep breath, and looked up. With a shock, he realized he was *there*. The corner of Begonia Street. The last place he'd seen his little brother.

A movement caught his eye. Something familiar. Then he heard his daughter's voice.

"Look what Uncle Bobby gave me!"

Half a block away, Marcy and Alana were walking down the street, Alana swinging her bag of loot. They were walking away from a large house.

Harlow's house. The giant, old monstrosity that had been dilapidated when he was a boy. It was still dilapidated, but strangely looked a little different. He hurried to it. Neither his wife nor daughter heard him or turned around. He wanted to call out, but his chest constricted and he couldn't breathe. In a moment. they were around the next corner.

The rage and grief of twenty years boiled over. Angry, bitter, and drunk, he slammed a fist on the broken front gate. It fell off its hinge.

I guess that's an invitation, he told himself, and went through. He banged on the front door.

"Harlow!" he shouted. "Open up! Time to answer for whatever you did, old man!" He pounded and pounded, but all he heard were echoes.

"I'll find you, old man. Uncle Bobby! What are you playing at?" he muttered as he worked his way through the overgrowth around the side of the house. "Hiding in your pumpkin patch again? Is that where you left my brother's body?"

He hadn't realized, but dusk was coming down. It was only late afternoon, but this time of year, it was pitch-dark before five o'clock. Something in the back of his mind told him he shouldn't be in this place when darkness fell, but his alcohol-fueled rage overruled any sane judgment. He plunged into the back garden.

It was just more overgrowth, the vegetable patch dead and weedy.

Pumpkin patch, he thought. And it became his driving thought. Brambles tore his shirt, scratched his face and hands, but he pushed through until he stood at the edge of the patch. It was lush and full of pumpkins, just like it had been every year he remembered when Bobby was still around.

Bobby. All Kevin's self-control went right out as he kicked the pumpkin nearest him, bashing it to seed and mush. He stomped, he raged, he didn't care if anyone saw him. Darkness fell, and he swung his leg again but this time caught it in a vine. He struggled to free it but lost his balance and went over backward, hard. The ground knocked the wind out of him.

He lay there on his back, struggling to catch his breath. He reached out to get a handhold and pull himself up but instead grabbed a smashed pumpkin. He pulled his hand away, sticky liquid all over it.

Gross, he thought. They're rotten.

He struggled to sit up but kept getting more tangled. He couldn't see what was wrapped around his ankle in the darkness.

"Need a hand?"

He started violently.

"What? Who's there?"

"It's me, the proprietor. You're trespassing, son."

"Harlow?" said Kevin, almost unbelieving. Almost. After today...

"You woke the pumpkins."

Kevin pulled himself into a sitting position and stared at the figure in front of him. It was the shape of Harlow, but the voice...

"Bobby?"

"We've been just fine here. Me and the pumpkins. You went away, Kevin. You left me, and now here I am." said the Bobby-thing. He leaned closer and Kevin recoiled, the stench of old, cold earth wafting off him, the distorted jack o' lantern rictus overlying his baby brother's features. "Why'd you come back? For Dad? Leave him alone. I'll take care of him."

"What the hell is going on?" said Kevin. He was sobering up, and part of his mind kept saying that this was some sort of Halloween trick. But who would trick him here? Who even knew he was here? He'd been gone for hours.

"Alana..."

"Oh, she's safe. The pumpkins only like boys." There was a long pause while the bizarre Harlow-pumpkin-Bobby thing stood and looked behind him. Kevin tried weakly to free himself, too terrified now to think. The creature turned back to him. "Too bad you're not a boy anymore," he—it said.

"Ow!" Kevin cried as his hand connected with something sharp. "What... Ow!" Something bit his foot.

"You woke them up. They're hungry." The old man knelt and peered into Kevin's face. Kevin whimpered.

Bobby.

Pumpkin Bobby on Harlow's body.

There was a rustle, then Kevin saw the pumpkins *move*.

Eyes. Fangs.

Kevin screamed as the bloody vampiric pumpkins tore into his flesh. He thrashed, but only sank deeper into the bloody pumpkin mush that was devouring him, slowly, but thoroughly. Some part of his mind tried begging, but all that escaped his throat were screams until one particularly vicious gourd opened wide, showing rows of fangs a shark might envy, and ripped out his throat clean to the spinal cord.

Gaping, eyes fading, Kevin succumbed. The pumpkins feasted.

The Harlow-pumpkin-Bobby thing stood and shook its head. "Hope you can come back. If you're not too old," it said.

***

One Year Later

Marcy, Alana, and Clara stood by the graveside after the funeral. Harvey had finally passed quietly. Just before he died, he'd murmured a grateful goodbye to them and then something incomprehensible to Bobby and Kevin, ghosts only he could see. He died thinking all of them were there with him.

As they left the cemetery, Alana stopped and pointed. "Daddy!" she cried.

But when they all turned to look, there was just the dirty shirt on the back of an old man turning the corner. Alana ran after him, ignoring the calls of her mother and grandmother.

"Daddy!" she cried, panicking. She was too little to have lost so much, and she knew, she just *knew* if she could reach that old *man*, she could get *something* back. Her eyes blurred from unshed tears, her feet tripped and stumbled over the cracked, uneven sidewalk, but she kept going, kept that dirty old shirt in front of her until he reached the old Harlow house, the forbidden house, the one that daddy was so afraid of last year. The stairs groaned and the porch boards creaked as he stepped on them.

"Daddy!" she cried again, arms out in front of her, stumbling and crying. She collapsed, a jagged, broken piece of sidewalk catching her tights. Her left knee caught the brunt, rough concrete skinning it bright red. "Daddy," she gasped.

His jack o' lantern rictus face turned to her. Her father's face was distorted but still recognizable and infinitely sad. He shook his head once and held his hands in front of him, signaling her to stop. She stopped, though her expression was still pleading.

He reached in his pocket and pulled out a box of long wooden matches. With great effort, he managed to croak out a few syllables.

"Go back to your mommy. Take her and grandma far, far away, and never tell them what you saw." He struck the match on the porch rail. The abrupt scent of sulfur struck her, and she watched the flame flare up and down before he tossed the match through the front window. The sulfur stench faded, replaced by the smell of woodsmoke. Papers and twigs. He'd prepared for this, planned it, and even wanted to show her. She choked on her sobs, trying to absorb what he wanted her to understand. They held each other's eyes until she began to calm and he was sure she accepted what she had to do. He forced one more awkward smile, a terrifying sight, then disappeared inside the house. She stood frozen, her mind ripping back and forth between obeying and running after him. She was very nearly about to put one foot forward when a loud crash of bursting glass followed by a blast of dust, ash, and sparks launched her a foot off the boards. She half ran, half scrabbled away from the disintegrating house. Soon, the entire property was a conflagration. Sirens sounded.

The townspeople came out to watch as the fire department fought to bring it under control. Their words floated over Alana's head like shifting clouds.

"Been a firetrap for years."

"Can't believe Harlow survived all these years to go down in flames."

"Was he inside?"

Alana glanced up sharply. A neighbor, who looked like every other neighbor, was looking at her. She nodded, not trusting her voice. Hands grabbed her from behind, and she allowed herself to be pulled back into her mother's embrace.

"Oh, honey. I'm so sorry. But that wasn't daddy. He's gone, sweetie."

Fresh tears fell from Alana's eyes onto her mother's shoulder as she forced a nod. He *was* gone. The difference was, Alana knew now where he'd gone. The roar of the fire behind them was the funeral dirge for Kevin Burkitt, a song only she could hear.

But she hadn't forgotten his message. "Mommy, I want to leave here. I don't ever, ever want to come back," she sniffled into her mother's hair. It smelled faintly of shampoo and hadn't yet been sullied with smoke-stink. Marcy gathered her child and her mother-in-law and hurried to the car.

As Marcy tucked Alana into the backseat, securing her seatbelt, the fire drafted over the long backyard, igniting the old pumpkin patch. A demonic roar, a sound like a thousand screaming souls, boomed over the crowd. The house tumbled down into mass rubble, and the crowd fled, crying and screaming the names of all the children that had gone missing, every Halloween, in the old Harlow pumpkin patch. It went on for what seemed like an eternity for scant moments before it finally went out. Extinguished, as if it had burned itself out completely, as if a mass grave had cried itself to sleep.

For years after, the neighbors nodded to one another knowingly, how the house had been a firetrap for far too long. Thank goodness it went out before it spread. They had said all these things before they retreated back into their dull, grey lives.

All that was left of the old house was dirt and rubble. Save for one little piece of pumpkin patch, far in the back, lush and loamy, with a tiny green sprout poking out.

* * *

The Third Father

By A. M. Todd

It wasn't until Russell's house went silent that he realized how much he depended on the usual noise. When it was quiet, nothing drowned out those sounds from outside: the voices shouting somewhere out in the night. *Must be more of those teenagers getting drunk in the fields*, Russell thought. He shook his head.

Why had his house gone quiet? It took a moment to register. Abby had stopped making noise. She sat on the living room carpet playing like always, whacking a book on the floor like she wanted to kill it dead, but in the past little while, she'd stopped squealing. That just wasn't like her. Russell crossed the living room, picked up his one-year-old daughter, and touched her forehead.

It was a little warm.

Russell paced the apartment, cradling Abby to his chest. He touched her forehead again. Still only a bit warm. She was fine, wasn't she? Should he take her for a check-up at the hospital, just to be sure? It was late, but the thought of leaving it until morning made his insides feel as though they'd been burned raw by acid.

Russell glanced through the window at the night outside. Dead leaves slapped quietly against the glass, swept up by the wind. The open air, cold and damp, wouldn't help Abby if she had a fever. Maybe he should call Dad. He'd know what to do. Putting Abby down, Russell reached for his phone, but as he picked it up, the sight of his daughter's pale blue eyes forced a new thought into his mind. It was a question he hated, one that haunted him whenever things didn't feel quite right—when he worried about something he'd said or done or whether Abby was safe.

Did Abby look like him?

The thought hung like a dead thing in his mind as he watched his daughter crawl along the floor. She was pale and chubby like her parents, but it was her hair and eyes that tormented Russell. He and Jessica both had dark brown hair—he remembered Jessica's hair like he'd seen it yesterday, long and thick and tangled on top of her head when she woke up in the morning. And both Russell and Jessica had brown eyes to match. Yet, here was Abby with her hair so blonde it was almost white and those bright gray eyes, pale gray like the bones in an X-ray.

Russell picked up his phone and called his father.

"How's Abby?" his father asked.

"Well, I'm not sure—I wanted to ask you about her." He paused. He'd planned to ask about taking her to the hospital, but suddenly he needed to set his mind to rest about that question. It ate away at him and made him feel raw.

"Russell," his father said. There was a brief pause. "What's this about?"

"Look, Dad," Russell said hesitantly, "you think Abby—you think she looks like me?"

Silence came from the phone, and more wild shouts from outside. Those drunks. The sounds reverberated in Russell's head, tormenting him.

"Russell, what are you doing, going at this again?" his father asked.

"Just answer the question, Dad."

"You asked me the same question yesterday. Why do you keep on asking me the same questions, over and over? She looks like you just fine, I told you."

"I keep on wondering about it, is all."

"It's bad enough that Jessica's gone and that girl's got to grow up without a mother. Now all you can do is make sure you raise that girl right, understand? You raise her right."

"I'm raising her right." Russell's voice was louder now.

"You taking her to church?"

"I can't believe you'd even ask me that. Of course I am."

"That girl needs a father who's not afraid to make decisions, lead the way for his child."

"I make decisions fine." Even as Russell said it, he knew it wasn't true. His whole life, he'd lingered in anguish over every choice: whether he should propose to Jessica even though they were so young, whether he should start a career at Arwell's, the pipe factory that employed half the town, including his father. What if his choice was the wrong one?

"Abby doesn't need a father who's always hesitating and asking the same questions over and over," his father said.

"Aw, Jesus Christ, Dad—"

"Don't swear where that child can hear you!"

"Fine!" Russell hung up. He felt a tinge of guilt about taking the Lord's name in vain, but his father had deserved it—Russell had only said it to annoy him. His father was nothing but a leech he'd never been able to get off him since childhood. Russell no longer wanted to ask him about taking Abby to the hospital, not after what he'd said about how Russell couldn't make decisions. Russell's hands shook at the idea of making a choice, but he forced himself onwards. He was a man and he could act by himself, so help him God. The doctor's office would be closed, but the town hospital would still be open.

When he went to pick up Abby, he found her lying on her back, the book beside her. Her feet and hands were bouncing softly, but they moved slower than usual. She let out a faint wail.

He scooped her up. "Abby, what's the matter?"

She began to cry, and a red flush had spread across her face. He touched her forehead and flinched. She was burning up. Just a minute ago she'd been only a little warm.

Moving fast, Russell dressed Abby in her winter hat and coat and carried her outside. He shivered as his rubber boots crunched on the twigs, cigarette butts, and leaves strewn across the driveway. Holding Abby in one arm, he fumbled for his keys. He fumbled and fumbled until both pockets had been turned inside out. Nothing.

He stifled a curse. What was going on? He thought he'd put his keys in his pocket, and his phone and wallet too.

All four car doors were locked. He crunched through the leaves back to the front door, but as he reached for the doorknob, his heartbeat quickened. He had no keys, and he'd locked the door from inside. Dad had always reprimanded him for losing things, told him he was thoughtless.

Helplessly, he tried the knob. Abby started crying again, her wails ringing out loud and lonely in the empty fields around them. Three times, he walked slowly back and forth from his door to the car, retraced his steps, searched the ground for his keys. Maybe he should break a window to go inside and get them. But no—what was he thinking? That was crazy. The gas station was only a two-minute walk down the road. He'd walk there and call Dad, and Dad would pick them up and take them to the hospital.

Ahead of them lay a familiar long, dirt road. No streetlights until the main street, not on a back road like this. A stretch of darkness separated Russell's house from the yellow light shining in the distance below the nearest streetlamp. Next to that light stood the gas station. Enclosed in its circle of yellow, that street corner looked distant, like a model town behind a glass display case, one of those miniature scenes displayed in museums. The streetlamp was a toothpick, the gas station a rectangle cut from cardboard.

The air smelled of manure and the current of the brook hissed in the background as Russell set out down the road, his daughter in his arms. It was cold, but Abby kept his shoulder warm. Sound travelled quickly in the open air. Abby's cries hurtled out into the dark, and the empty fields took the sounds and smothered them. Somewhere in the distance, wings flapped as a bird took flight.

"Things are just fine, Abby," Russell said. "That's the gas station right up there."

Moonlight fell, bare and ugly, on the countryside lining the road.

Dirt and debris, pools of dark water, and metal scraps lying jagged in the grass. The lines of the fence, with its wooden poles impaling the air, hung sharp and crooked in the sky like teeth. Those geometric lines stood out against the softer lines of the wild, unruly life that grew behind them. Between the scraps of metal, holes opened onto pockets of dirt and the unclean life that grew in them. Fungus. Weeds. Pools of standing water where creatures lived and grew. Russell could smell it. He knew that reek like nothing else. He passed the remains of an old driveway that branched off the side of the road. One night he'd walked by and seen a car parked in that driveway: Daniel Saunders' old Chevrolet with the Praise Jesus bumper sticker. When Russell had walked past the back door, he'd seen nothing but a man's bare ass with a woman's legs wrapped around it. That sure hadn't been Daniel's wife in there. Church-going Lisa Saunders wouldn't be caught dead in a car like that. Russell always tried not to think about loose people like that, the ones who didn't care about their marriage vows, who reproduced like weeds. They reminded him of all the life that grew and festered out in the fields, the filth he wanted nothing to do with.

Abby wailed. Russell had almost forgotten about her even though he was holding her. He ought to do better, he told himself. She was his child after all, his blood and kin. Once or twice, when Abby had been very young, Russell had gone into another room and completely forgotten his child's existence. He had to remind himself to be more careful about that.

Above the quiet hiss of the brook, a new sound rose in the dark. The sound of shoes walking on dirt. Russell stopped moving, but the noise continued behind him. He looked over his shoulder.

In the distance, near his house, stood a thin sliver that looked like a human silhouette. It had stopped walking and stood motionless. Russell froze, clutching Abby tightly. Instinct coiled up inside him like a spring. He was ready to run, to hide, maybe in the long grass lining the road.

But as he looked more closely at that sliver of blue, he realized it wasn't moving. It might not be a person after all. His house, all its windows black, formed a vague rectangle of shadow in the distance, and that vertical streak of blue appeared blurry and indistinct, as though it might be part of the dark shape behind it.

Russell kept walking, his feet moving faster now. The laughter of those drunks echoed out in the fields, and it felt as though the sounds were all around him, pressing in on him.

It had begun again: shoes crunching on dirt. Russell turned. There, twenty feet back, stood a tall, thin man in a navy-blue suit. He stood still with his arms hanging lifelessly at his sides like a dormant puppet. Russell couldn't make out his face, but he had familiar white-blond hair, parted straight down the middle.

Adrenaline sharpened the lines, textures, and colors around Russell. He knew who that man was. It was a man he'd seen before, many times.

***

About two years ago, Russell spent an afternoon isolated in his study, eager to lose himself building his model factory. He worked on it whenever he wanted to forget the tense quiet in his house, the little needling remarks and the stiff neck he got from sleeping on the couch every night. The model factory made that disappear.

As Russell glued another beam onto the ceiling of the model, the tightness in his chest gave way to the joy of the work: the meticulous care, precision, control. He'd built model towns his whole life, but this factory fascinated him more than any other. It was built to look like Arwell's, the pipe factory where his father worked. Russell had been eight years old the first time he'd visited Arwell's. He remembered it vividly: the finished pipes had been piled up in clusters around the sides, the ends looking like a honeycomb—and from the moment he'd stepped inside Arwell's, the sight of the pipes had filled him with awe. Soon they would be exported to sewage systems all over the country. In

Russell's mind, the pipes were a picture of efficiency. They shuttled away all the filth, into the gutters and out of sight. They hid the unclean and left pure, untainted water in its place. And Russell had been in awe of the men who worked at Arwell's, too—the men who operated the machinery, bent the metal to their will, cut the pipes with fire. They were the men Russell's father admired so much, who did their jobs and kept things quiet, the men who—like his father said—"made things run like they should."

Russell's eyes fell on one of the finished model pipes near the edge of the table: it was sticking out awkwardly, as though someone had bumped it walking by. *How hideous*, Russell thought. He snatched the pipe and examined it. It was broken, a piece chipped off one end, leaving a gaping hole in the pipe. It was unbearable. Horrifying. Pipes were meant to keep things separate, to keep certain things out and other things in. Russell couldn't stand that imperfection in the factory. His father's words passed through his head: "If something's wrong, you fix it. You deal with it."

But Russell didn't want to fix it. He didn't even want to look at it long enough to repair it; he would rather not think of at it all. Fixing it would be messy work. It would mean becoming one with the mess, if only for a little while, and this frightened him. It revolted him: the thought of mingling two things that should be separate.

Instead, he put the broken piece away in a drawer. Relief came over him as he hid the flaw from sight.

The study door opened. "Hiding stuff in drawers again?" Jessica asked. Once, she'd gone looking for something in the study and found the drawers overflowing with things Russell had hidden there.

Russell didn't answer.

She looked through the contents of the drawer: broken pieces of papier-mâché, a blade with no handle, a rusted copper plate, a miniature forklift. She sighed. "More of this? Why don't you just leave the broken pieces out on the desk? You know I keep important documents in the drawers. Look at this—you got paint on one of them."

"Sorry."

"Just leave them out," she said again, taking the broken pipe and putting it on the desk, next to the model.

Jessica came closer, hovering behind him, but he kept his attention fixed on the factory. "Look," she said, "I know I got mad earlier, but we should talk about some of that shit we said this morning."

"I hate when you swear like that."

"At least tell me what's been bothering you lately. You've been so on edge."

There were many things bothering him. He tried to focus on one of the issues, to put it into words, so he could talk about it. But the very idea of thinking clearly about those nasty things—he couldn't bear it. To give them names and words would make them real.

Instead, he turned back to the factory. Jessica hovered for a little longer, then exhaled a long, heavy breath of air and left the study. The second she was gone, Russell placed the broken pipe back in the drawer and shut it tight.

Later that day, he and Jessica fought. Russell said terrible things. Jessica left the house, and she was gone all night. He tried her phone. Her friends' phones. In the morning he was ready to go to the police, but suddenly the door opened and there she was, her eyes sleepy and lips stained with red wine. She never told him where she went.

About a month later, Jessica told Russell she was pregnant. But when the baby came, something unthinkable happened. Jessica died in childbirth. Russell was left alone with a beautiful child with white-blonde hair and eyes the color of X-rays.

But when Russell saw that baby, doubts sprouted like weeds in his mind. In a nightmare that tormented him again and again, he entered the room with Abby's crib to find a man standing beside it, his back turned Russell and his white-blond hair parted straight down the middle. "Who are you?" Russell asked. The man turned to face him, but he had a red cloth over his face. The cloth seemed to be attached to nothing, just stuck there clinging to his skin. They stood staring at one another for what felt like hours, until finally Russell asked again, "Who are you?" The man reached up and slowly pulled the cloth away from his face. There they were: those distinct, pale gray eyes like Abby's, eyes that made Russell choke with fear. The man turned again and picked Abby up, and how similar the two of them looked, how natural and happy she seemed in his arms. Russell stood, paralyzed, as the stranger took the baby and left. The dream repeated endlessly, and every time it was the same: the moment the man revealed his face, that was when he took the baby.

Sometimes, after those dreams, Russell felt a strong need to act. He needed to do something, anything to be certain. He would often hold Abby in front of the mirror, staring at the two faces looking back: did she look like him? He would spend hours like this—maybe with the right lighting, or a better angle, he would see the resemblance in a cheekbone or jawline. He would also ask his father whether Abby looked like him. And sometimes, after a night when the dreams were especially vivid, he even found himself on his computer, trying to log in to Jessica's social media accounts, or her emails and instant messages. He hated himself for doing it, but he had to be certain. He just had to be certain. If he could see her messages from around *that time*, then maybe he could put all this to rest and move on. But he never managed to get into any of her accounts. After all those years of marriage, he still couldn't guess her password.

***

A year later, Russell stood with Abby in his arms on the way to the gas station, staring back at the blond man who had appeared by his house. Abby had stopped crying and rested on his shoulder. The skin of her forehead burned against his neck. Her fever was getting worse.

"Leave us alone," Russell called back in a shaking voice. "I don't have money or a wallet or anything you want."

No response came. The man stood impossibly still. How could this be? Russell had only seen this man in his head. It was impossible that he could be standing here. And yet, Russell was sure he wasn't dreaming.

Russell took a few more steps toward the gas station. It was close, just a minute ahead. But the moment he turned his back on the man, the footsteps started again. The stalker was playing some sick game. And why couldn't Russell make out his face? The man was close enough, but his face appeared only as a blur in Russell's mind. Russell sensed that if he focused for long enough, he could make out those features, but he did not want to see that face.

He must not see that face.

The thought sliced into him as the images from his dream crowded his mind. The moment he saw that face, the man would take the baby.

Suddenly Russell was running, feet coming down hard against the dirt, Abby heavy in his arms. The jolting movement made her shriek. As he ran, the world around him changed. Sounds grew louder. The crickets whined in the fields. The brook roared with movement. And the shoes crunched behind him. The sounds deafened him—that brook, the crickets, the frogs, the life thriving out in the fields. He ran until his lungs seared.

The shoes scuffed against the dirt. Russell reached the gas station. The yellow light of the streetlamp surrounded him. Chest heaving, he held Abby in one arm and reached for the door handle. He tugged on it, but it wouldn't give. Locked.

The gas station was closed. It must close early on Sunday evening.

Unsteadily, Russell stepped backwards. Through the window he saw the dark interior of the station, the shadowy shapes of shelves. Behind him, the sound of shoes on dirt became the sound of shoes on pavement. And in the reflection on the window, the image of a man in a navy-blue suit grew steadily larger.

Russell's head pounded with terror. Abby's small hands clutched at his shoulder. He looked behind him. Just six feet away, the stalker stood tall, faceless, and thin as one of the weeds that grew out behind Russell's house. The wind whipped into him, but his suit and slacks didn't move. Behind him was the edge of the yellow light from the streetlamp, and beyond that, the wide emptiness of the fields, one pool of standing water gleaming in the moonlight. Russell realized, in the back of his mind, that if his father had been here, his father would've confronted that man.

But not Russell. Instead, he clung to Abby with white, freezing hands and sprinted north in the direction of the hospital, the sidewalk flying under his feet and Abby's cries ringing out shrill and helpless. Streetlamps streaked by, but the sides of the road were empty, nothing but the fields behind them. No cars passed. The man's steps shadowed him.

Russell stumbled. He needed to calm down. He needed to focus so he could defend his daughter. Closing his eyes, he recalled a memory that calmed him when he was anxious. Tall ceilings vaulted above the interior of his father's steel pipe factory. He thought of the men who kept things quiet and in order, who made things run like they should. He thought of the pipes that would keep the town clean.

Within a few seconds, the memory had calmed him, filled him with strength. His shaking subsided. He opened his eyes.

The man was gone.

As Russell slackened his pace, Abby stopped crying. "Oh God," he said. "Abby, we're gonna be okay. Look, I see the hospital now."

Some distance ahead, the rectangular brick walls of the hospital stood by the side of the road. Lights shone behind the windows and there were cars in the parking lot. Russell could hear a car engine starting, traffic moving in the distance. And faintly, voices talking as two distant figures headed from the hospital back to their car.

Russell kissed the top of Abby's white-blonde head. "We're okay," he said. His sweat dried and froze on his forehead. The hospital came closer.

It started slowly, but it grew steadily. The sound of footsteps.

"Goddamn you!" Russell cried.

Again, he recalled the image of the factory, held it vividly in his mind, but when he turned around, the man was still there. Only when he imagined it a second time, and for longer, did the man disappear again.

But when Russell kept walking, the footsteps started again. Abby's breathing rustled in his ear, and her nose ran on his shoulder. Her face burned. He tried to walk backwards, watching the stalker so he had to stand still, but Russell couldn't bear the sight of him, the fear that he might see that man's face. Again, he thought of the factory. This time he had to imagine it three times.

"My girl is sick," he pleaded over his shoulder when the man appeared again. "Please, just let me take her to the hospital. She's burning up."

No reply came. The man's breathing shuddered behind him.

Russell touched Abby's forehead. Even hotter than a few minutes ago. Running wasn't working. But what else could he do? He thought about what the men at the factory would do right now. What his father would do. They would confront this stalker. They would smash his face, shove him to the ground, put their hands around his throat and squeeze until they felt his windpipe collapse, until they'd squeezed the sin right out of him and it seeped out into the gutter where it belonged, swept away into the pipes.

But no, Russell thought, he shouldn't do that. What if the man was dangerous? What if confronting him endangered Abby? He needed a third option.

Looking at that man reminded Russell of the dread he felt when he looked at the hideously flawed, broken pieces in his model factory. The ones he'd hidden in the drawer. His father would tell him to fix them, but Russell would rather put them away. But he remembered what Jessica had said about the broken pieces, her voice strained with the effort of smoothing things over after their last fight: "Just leave them out."

Leave them out, he thought. It felt impossible. Just leave that man there and don't try to get rid of him? Let him get closer and closer until he breathed hot, sickening breath on the back of Russell's neck? Until his face came into focus? The decision felt like rusty metal gears being wrenched from their normal circuits; Russell felt himself forcing his mind to turn in new ways as the trajectory of his thoughts changed, like a circle being forced into a new shape.

He drew his breath in sharply. Slowly, he forced himself to turn around, his pulse thundering. The stalker stood, now unmoving, a foot away. The wrinkles on the shoulders of his suit appeared in clear detail, like the brown leather belt he wore, the veins on the hands that hung limply at his sides. And yet his face was still a blur in Russell's mind.

Russell longed to call to mind the factory and make the man go away, but this time, he forced himself to look, deeply and clearly, at the man's face. Slowly, as if a layer of film was being peeled away, the stalker's features began to slide into focus from the top down. First the smooth, pale skin of his forehead. Then the thick yellow eyebrows shining in the electric light, the terrifying, intense eyes, the long nose and chin. But it was those eyes that Russell fixated on. Big and gray like the color of an X-ray.

Russell stood frozen. He felt faint. How his daughter looked a lot like that man. That face threatened to make him come undone. That face destroyed everything the factory meant to him; it ripped the memory to tatters, its scraps falling like feathers in a zig-zag motion until they hit the mud.

Russell and the man stared at one another. Neither spoke. Leaves rustled in the background as the wind lifted up dead matter and scattered it across the landscape. But Russell, as he stood there shaking like a frightened child, did not confront the man. Instead, he did nothing.

It was a simple nothing, cold and unwelcoming, a blankness that rose up inside him and stifled his deep, desperate desires to either run or confront. The nothing was not a resignation, but it wasn't a confrontation either. It was the nothing that he knew best, the one he'd practiced his whole life—the indecision, the inaction, the place in between one choice and another.

He turned his back on the man and kept walking. But now he moved at a normal pace, slow and steady. He no longer tried to escape.

Relentlessly, those brown dress shoes clicked on the sidewalk behind him, but he did nothing about it. The man breathed hot, sickening air onto the back of his head, but he did nothing about it. And the man did not take the baby.

The man followed and followed. Russell reached the sliding doors and hurried inside with Abby, and in the waiting room, people's eyes passed over the stranger as if they saw right through him. No one acknowledged his presence.

"My daughter's got a fever," Russell said anxiously to the lady at the reception desk.

It didn't take long before a nurse led him into a room and the doctor came. As she examined Abby, Russell glanced behind her and saw the man standing in the doorway. Since he'd forced himself to look clearly, the stranger's face appeared in lucid detail—not blurry and unfocused like it used to be—and Russell could see those distinctive, pale gray eyes.

Later that night, Russell took Abby home, and the stranger had disappeared. Those drunken shouts still echoed outside, but they were fainter now.

***

The next day, Russell kept a close eye on Abby, even though the doctors were never in doubt: her fever had subsided and she looked perfectly healthy, if a little fussy from the night's ordeals. He sat with her and read their favorite book, and he didn't stand in front of the mirror to look for the resemblance between them, not even once.

In the evening, he walked into the living room and jumped. The blond man was standing behind the window. Russell's body tightened.

He wanted to shut the curtains and block him out. But he remembered what he'd done the night before, and his wife's advice. *Just let it be there.*

He forced himself not to close the window. He would let the man stand there. He would neither block him out, nor confront him; he would simply let him be. And eventually, the man disappeared.

Over the next few weeks, sometimes, the man appeared outside Russell's windows, or off in the distance in the fields. But if Russell just let him be there, he went away in time. As the days passed, Russell found himself comparing Abby's and his reflections in the mirror less often. And he called his father less to ask him questions.

One afternoon, Russell was rummaging through the storage room and came across a side table he hadn't used in years. In one of its drawers, he found an old phone. He recognized the blue plastic case: one of Jessica's old phones, perhaps two years old now. Russell picked it up, plugged it in to charge it, and turned it on. He was surprised to find the phone unlocked; Jessica had always been so careful about these things. He opened her inbox.

There they were. All her text messages, including messages from *that time.* He stood silently in the attic, its rafters straining under the weight of old secrets. If he wanted certainty, he could have it. His hands shook.

Instead, summoning all his self-control, he powered down the phone without reading any messages. He carried it back into the kitchen, opened the cupboard beneath the sink, and threw it in the garbage.

He sat down to steady himself. Now he could never be certain. But maybe he didn't need to be certain after all. If he felt uncertain, sometimes he might see that man outside his window, but if he did, now he knew what to do. He could just let him be there.

Russell went to Abby's crib, picked her up, and held her. Yes, she did have very blue eyes, but maybe they came from a great aunt, or some family member he never knew. He let the uncertainty wrap around him, sharp and fresh, an almost welcome feeling.

* * *

Troop 94's Last Scouting Trip

By Karl Melton

When I was seven, I dreamed of sailing the seas as a dread pirate like Henry Morgan. At nine, I wanted to be a fisherman in Alaska, where I would capture the largest King Salmon ever recorded. At twelve, I was hell-bent on joining the Navy the second I graduated high school. A year later, at thirteen, I promised myself I would never set foot on a boat again.

For ten years I've stayed true to my promise, avoiding beaches, boats, and the briny deep sea. All because of what happened a decade earlier, when Boy Scouts Troop 94 stayed overnight on the USS *Hornet*.

Dad was Troop Leader and lone adult chaperone. With scheduling conflicts and an overnight commitment, it wasn't exactly a well-attended event, but I didn't care. I had my best friend Paul with me. Paul and I were inseparable. We spent every second of the two-hour drive together in the back seat of my Dad's Jeep, eyes glued to our dim Nintendo DS screens. Just as the low battery notification flashed, we pulled into a large, industrial harbor.

Once the other scouts arrived, we walked toward the great steel hull that was half-shrouded in the dense, low-hanging fog in the distance. Gulls swarmed above and disappeared into the horizon, leaving us with the fading sound of their squawking and wailing. As we got to the docks, the aircraft carrier in all its glory manifested itself. Buzzing anticipation formed in the pit of my stomach. The idea of staying overnight on the legendary *Hornet* had dominated my thoughts ever since they announced the trip a month prior.

As I stood admiring the steel giant, an older man with a graying flat top haircut walked toward us. He was wearing a blue polo that read *USS*

Hornet, 1943-1970. Heritage of Excellence.

"Ah, this must be Troop 94," the man said. "My name is Howard, and for the next sixteen odd hours, I'll be your tour guide. Looks like you all brought your sleeping bags, so follow me and I'll show you the crew living quarters." He glanced at his watch. "I'm afraid you're a tad late, but we can cut into dinner. Shouldn't be a problem."

As we did our best to keep up with Howard's brisk pace, I looked back at Dad. He raised his hands in a shrug, as if to say, *What can you do? Traffic is traffic.* Dad always was more laid-back than other adults.

At least, that's what Mom always said. I don't think she liked that about Dad. Especially after he lost his office job. A few months ago, she picked me up at school and took me to Pizza Palace. I ate like a king, swallowing mouthfuls of hot pepperoni and cheese. But I had a feeling she was hiding something. Later that night when she told me to sit on the couch, I *knew* she was hiding something.

"Honey, you know Dad and I love each other very much right?"

"Yeah," I had said, my voice a whimper.

"Well, sometimes... when you love each other you decide to do what's best for the family..."

Sharp pain shot through my toe as my mind returned to the ship. Not two minutes into my *Hornet* adventure and I had already kicked hard metal in a raised open doorway, nearly stumbling in the process. My cheeks turned hot as I tried to regain composure.

"You kids ain't on land anymore. Remember that, and get your bearings," Howard said. We left our luggage near the bunks and returned to Howard and Dad in the hanger bay.

"Hey, boys, gather around," Dad said. "Howard here will give you boys a tour. I gotta step out and file some paperwork, so act like the saints I know you all are and don't cause any trouble, okay? I don't want a repeat of the Sly Park disaster." He pointed at me. "Keep an eye on Hunter over there. He's always the instigator."

His pep talk over, Dad left the hangar while we let out bursts of suppressed snickering. Howard forced a wry smile and started the tour, leading us from the large open spaces of the hanger deck to the cramped passageways of the 2nd deck. The place was a time capsule. An operating table in the sick bay was prepped with clean white sheets. Bibles were scattered about in the chapel, and an old rotary phone sat on a desk in the officer's stateroom.

Despite the antiquated mid-20th century furniture and equipment, the place seemed like a living, breathing station of war, as if at any moment hundreds of men returning from leave would storm the various bays and engine rooms, and set sail to bring the enemies of America to their heels. A bolt of excitement ran through my body as I imagined myself commanding a ship just like the *Hornet*, only bigger, newer, and with *a lot* more guns.

We moved on to the flight deck three levels above. Gun mounts larger than cannons pointed their 50 caliber-long barrels toward the foggy waters of the San Francisco Bay. Several aircraft were on display, including an F-11 Tiger interceptor with a bright orange paint job of a shark's mouth on the front fuselage.

As we wrapped up, Paul swerved from side to side like a little kid with a full bladder. Howard made eye contact, and Paul said the words that must have been burning on his tongue for the past hour: "Is this ship haunted?"

Two other scouts, Robbie and Austin, erupted in laughter at the urgency of the question. Paul blushed, but waited for an answer.

"Yeah, Dad said this place might have ghosts," I said, hoping my enthusiasm would shut Robbie and Austin up.

Howard looked down and chuckled. "Now listen here, I've been part of the *Hornet* crew since '65. Enlisted right out of High School, not much older than you boys are now. Lord knows I've seen my fair share of strange happenings. Mostly pathetic pranks put on by rowdy teenagers, but I know this ship. It's not haunted. There's no such thing as ghosts." Howard's voice lingered as the crying gulls passed beyond the cloudy haze. "It's something else with this ship."

We strained our faces, waiting for Howard to clarify.

"Okay, look. I've told you everything I'm supposed to, so the tour is over."

We let out a groan as Howard continued.

"I imagine there's some good grub in the mess hall now, so let's get you boys fed and then we can get to any other... extracurricular questions."

***

The mess hall was a commotion of frenzied conversations as staff and scouts gathered to dine on spaghetti and salad. Paul and I sat next to Howard, eager to learn more from the vet.

"Let's get one thing straight," Howard said, raising a finger. "The *only* reason I'm telling you this is because you boys seem mature enough, and well, as a former Scout myself, I feel obligated to answer your questions. But if I hear one word about you two not being able to sleep, I won't be happy, which means you definitely won't be happy. You hear?"

I nodded and leaned forward, clasping my hands together on the table.

"All right, then. Let me ask you, boys. Why do you think they decommissioned the *Hornet* in 1970?"

"The ship was over 25 years old," I said.

Howard laughed. "Twenty-five years? That's nothing. This isn't Uncle Sam's Canoe Club. They didn't decommission the Midway until '92. For *45* years, that ship sailed the globe as four acres of sovereign U.S. soil. Now I might be biased and all, but I'll tell ya now for the longest time, the pride of the Navy was the *Hornet*. Not the Midway. During our glory days, we took down over a thousand Jap planes. *Our* pilots took the first strikes on Tokyo. In '69 it was the *Hornet* that recovered the astronauts of Apollo 11 and 12."

Paul's eyes lit up as he dropped his fork. "Wait, you guys picked up Neil Armstrong and Buzz Aldrin?"

"Yep. On this very ship."

"What were they doing here?" Paul asked.

"Twenty-one-day quarantine procedure. Merely precautionary. Back then, we just didn't know enough about any potential toxins they could have brought back. Let's see, that was my... fourth year in the crew, and well... you think there was cause for celebration, but that's when the real trouble began."

"Trouble. What trouble?" I asked.

"Officially, the recovery missions themselves were on paper a complete success. It was all that media attention that backfired. Let's go back to my question. Ask people why the Navy retired the *Hornet*, and most will repeat your answer about its age. Some say asbestos. Others ramble on about some budget nonsense. But I was on the *Hornet* in '69. When the suicides began."

Paul and I exchanged wide-eyed looks. The clinking and clanking of cheap silverware faded away as we gave our full attention to Howard's story.

"Now a ship our size always brushed with death, but it was bad that year. So bad, we ended up the reluctant recipient of the "highest suicide rate in the navy" award. The officers did all they could to control it. Even had a group of fresh-faced therapists on call for any guy feeling jumpy. It didn't stick... and Tom decided a midnight dive in the middle of the Pacific was preferable to whatever torments he faced on board. Poor guy." He paused, twisting his fork in his cold spaghetti. "I grew up with Tom. We both enlisted the same day. The guy handled stress so well. Always had a smile on his face, and a racy joke in his pocket for when things got too quiet. It just made no sense. No sense at all."

His voice drifted, and I felt an urge to fill the silence. "I'm sorry. What changed that year?"

"I ask myself that a lot. Could be a type of chain reaction, with each suicide driving down morale and causing the next person to jump. But I'm no therapist. I'm just the tour guide." He raised his glass to drink, realized it was empty, and collected his tray. "Picking up those astronauts changed things. It couldn't have been a coincidence. I can't not think about it, especially when I'm back here, trying to sleep on the same bunks Tom and I slept on for all those years. Just what did those moon men bring back with them?"

Paul was the first to speak. "Do you mean—"

"I didn't mean anything." Howard's face was red. His eyes cloudy. "Sorry, boys, you get old like me and you lose your train of thought and start talking rubbish that makes no sense. Like I said, I'm just the old tour guide with fading memories and nothing to do. Now get some rest, boys. No one sleeps in on the *Hornet*."

Paul and I sat alone at the corner of the table, trying to reconstruct Howard's history lesson. The rest of the night came and went. As I was walking toward the bunks, Dad called out.

"Hunter, hold on a sec. I'm not letting you off the hook that easy. Say goodnight to your old man."

I grinned and stuck my tongue out.

"You rascal. How was the tour?"

"It was good."

"Still sure the Navy life is for you?"

"More than ever."

"Good. I'm glad you got to experience this. I know these past few months have been rough on us all." His voice idled, and I realized he was no longer smiling. His eyes glazed over, as if he was thinking of something else.

Seeing my Dad act like... well, not— Dad, made me feel guilty. I leaned in for a hug, and he held me there with sweaty hands.

"Dad, can't you move back in?"

"We'll see. I think right now your Mom and I need a little space."

"Ok, Dad."

"Good night, Hunter. I love you."

I wished him the same and made my way to the crew's berthing, where several aisles of bunks stretched from port to starboard. The beds were stacked three high on either side and hung from the walls in heavy chains, creating a metallic jingling each time someone above or below shifted. I jumped in the bunk above Paul and closed my eyes. *Yeah, I can get used to this. Just a few more years and I'll actually be in the Navy.* The thought somehow felt forced. I wanted to believe it, but I found my brain thinking back to Howard. He had that look on his face adults sometimes get when they curse or say something about sex before realizing we heard them. *What were we not supposed to hear?* Just as sleep was about to take me, it came to me. The line I would think about for the rest of that night, and likely, the rest of my life.

Just what did those moon men bring back with them?

***

I gave up on sleeping soon after. My mind thought back to third grade when we learned about the moon landing. Mrs. Jones made it seem like there were just rocks up there, but I didn't think Howard was crazy enough to think this is all about some moon rocks. I made a mental note to talk to Paul about it sometime tomorrow when the noises started.

Creaks and groans reverberated throughout the old ship, creating a soundtrack of ambient noise my brain couldn't ignore. Eventually, the creaks were overshadowed by a thundering bang, as if the nearby hatches in the ship were opening and closing. I sat up, holding my breath deep in my lungs until I heard the booming noise again. Paul was tossing and turning in the bunk below me.

"Paul, are you awake?"

"I am now. What's that banging?" he whispered back.

"No idea. And at least you got some sleep. I've been up for hours."

Robbie and Austin woke from the nearest bunk and joined us. As the four of us deliberated, a sensation of vertigo swept over me. I looked at my friends and saw in their eyes. They noticed it too. A shift in equilibrium. My heart sank, submerged in a wave of panic. The carrier, decommissioned for over 30 years, was moving. *We* were moving.

Despite our shared confusion and alarm, we agreed not to overreact. The rest of the boys were asleep, so we decided to find Dad or Howard and let them take control. We left the crew's berthing with muted footsteps and made our way to the separate section of living quarters where adults and staff slept. While the room was dark, like ours, there was no snoring, rattling of chains, or even breathing. In fact, there were no adults at all. Only their luggage remained, lying on empty beds in the lifeless room.

A chill ran down my spine as we scoured the room again. No staff. No Dad. Just four boy scouts on the cusp of puberty, clueless and alone. Paul stayed the most composed.

"Just stop," he said. "Think! If the ship is moving, *someone* has to be navigating."

"The Island," I said. "Captain's Bridge."

Paul nodded. "That's probably where your Dad is. He woke up before us and went with Howard to investigate."

It made sense. Why would they wake us up and cause a commotion? If there was trouble, they wouldn't want us involved. We ventured out to explore the vast maze-like hallways of the floating city. With little light, none of us knew the direct path to the Island. But we knew what direction to head. Up. Up to the flight deck. Up to the Island.

We rounded a tight corridor and saw the path before us lit by the dim red glow of a nearby light. My feet froze as the sound echoed past us. Someone else was here. The clatter of heavy footsteps advanced on our position. Before we could react, the crimson light was extinguished and darkness flooded in.

The light was out for mere moments, yet when it returned, I counted only two others with me. Paul was *gone*. In unison we cried out to him, no longer worried about staying quiet. No response.

Unable to deal with the disappearance of both my Dad and best friend, I cracked. Tears flowed from weary eyes as the reality of the situation set in. When before we could explain the sensation of being in a moving ship to delusion, maintenance, or miscommunication, there was no mistaking what had occurred. No ignoring the bitter paradox that the three of us were without the other boys or adults, yet not alone.

The shameful temptation to backtrack and cower in the bunks took hold of me, but I resisted. *We* resisted, as both Robbie and Austin swore they would help find Paul.

The banging sound I last heard in bed returned. We followed it to a ladder and climbed, knowing it could be our only way to track Paul. Our ascent continued to the next level. We clung together, refusing to let a single inch separate the three of us. Sight proved little help as darkness swarmed us. We learned to trust our ears to register the shrill clang of nearby hatches opening. In one poorly lit corner of the hangar deck, Austin insisted he saw something move in the opposite direction and started to run toward it. Robbie and I held him back until he swore to not chase after dancing shadows. We had *one* goal, and we couldn't afford to lose focus. We sprinted toward the nearest stairwell. Sweat seeped from my pores and landed in the corner of my eyes. I wiped the moisture away and forced myself not to look back at whatever Austin claimed to see.

A cool gush of ocean air welcomed us as we reached the flight deck. We stepped through the heavy sea fog surrounding the ship and almost walked into an F-14 Tomcat on the landing strip. I grasped onto the cold, wet railing on the edge of the deck. With little to no visibility, I couldn't determine where we were, other than the obvious. Something set the *Hornet* free, and we were in the open ocean with no land in sight. The rough waters stirred with a force I have never seen before. I strained my eyes and saw a floating clump of white foam following the ship's stern with a steady pace. Nearby bubbles rose, rupturing on the surface of the dark water.

I leaned farther over the railing, trying to see more. *Needing* to see more. A clammy hand grasped my shirt and pulled me back. It was Robbie. His mouth opened in exaggerated movements, and as I lost focus on the crashing waves, I realized he was shouting we had no time. I nodded, taking in deep breaths.

The *Hornet's* Island rose from the middle of the flight deck. A steel giant, large enough to be a ship in its own right. An array of radar and radio antennas protruded from the top like a crown of spikes. At the base, a hatch was ajar, swaying and creaking in the ocean wind. We walked through. Austin moved to close the hatch behind him, but I reached for his arm and raised a finger to my lips. We made no noise. For the past few hours, we all felt the sensation that something or someone was stalking us in the shadows. But now, the roles shifted. Inside the Island, we listened as two distinct voices echoed down. One I recognized. The other completely alien to me.

I had never heard Dad cry before. His voice was a muddled mix of sobs and pleas. "I can't do it."

"You had no trouble throwing the first one over. Finish the job."

"Not to my boy!"

"You don't get to choose. *They* need to eat."

The voices faded in the background as I made my decision to climb. The ladder bars were slick, coated in sweat or something else entirely. I inched closer until I felt a foot give way and slip. In a panic, I kicked and scratched against the ladder until I regained my footing. No one spoke. I only heard the beating of my heart and the lingering, paralyzing silence.

The stranger, in his calm and authoritative voice, whispered something. A question. I couldn't make it out. He had no answer. Suddenly, there was commotion overhead. Weight shoved against sheet metal. Grunts and yells. Broken glass. I climbed, no longer worried about making noise. Robbie and Austin were moving below me, but I didn't wait. I pulled myself up and looked around the captain's bridge.

A cold draft filled the room as glass from the broken windows crunched below my sneakers. The bridge was empty. All I found was a bloody shard of glass lying on the green tile floor. A trail of blood led to the outside balcony. I leaned against the railing, towering over the landscape. What I saw was both impossible yet undeniable. The patch of fog had diminished, revealing expanding ripples in the water, and dozens of dark forms encircling it. At first, I suspected sharks, but these were smaller, with no dorsal fins. They moved fast, never penetrating the surface of the water. And while I couldn't be sure, their outlines looked more humanoid than fish. With unrelenting speed, they... feasted on something just below the water. By the time Robbie and Austin reached the railing, they were gone, replaced with that white foam I saw earlier, and the distant sirens of patrol boats.

***

The Coast Guard found all the staff drugged and locked away. The blood on the glass belonged to Dad, and his fingerprints were everywhere. There was only one suspect.

The papers found out and had a field day. *Suicidal father. Unemployed and disgruntled. Recently separated from wife*, and so on and so on. The case was open and shut, despite all the unknowns. There were no theories on how anyone could hijack the decommissioned carrier, where the ship was en route to, and why Search and Rescue recovered no bodies. They never took Robbie, Austin, and me seriously when we *insisted* we heard a second voice in the Island. Instead, we were met with medical words like *trauma*. We had to be *traumatized* after witnessing our much beloved Troop Leader commit murder-suicide, and our *traumatized* brains had to imagine something else to cope.

That night changed me. It changed a lot of the boys. The stinging pain of loss never truly went away. I felt it while watching two empty coffins being lowered in the ground. I felt it watching rage build in the eyes of adults as they launched accusations against a dad who couldn't defend himself. I felt it watching those same eyes turn to regret, as they told us they must disband Troop 94 due to complications with the search for a new Troop Leader. I felt it in the countless therapy sessions Mom sent me to. I feel it now.

That ambitious 13-year-old boy obsessed with dreams of Navy life and fighting wars in foreign wharf towns lost the war inside his own head. Very little of that boy exists in the broke, 24-year-old college student who is still 30 credits shy from graduating. Mom threatened to withhold tuition unless I "confront my demons." Something had to give, so I caved, and broke the promise I made to myself 11 years ago after Troop 94's last scouting trip.

The next morning, Mom and I drove to that industrial harbor I never wanted to see again. The skies were clear of both fog and seagulls. But the *Hornet* was still there, secured to the docks like it had never left. Waiting for me.

We walked in the crowded hangar deck, and something brushed against my back. It was Paul, the friend I lost so long ago. He looked at me with a blank stare, his shirt wet, red, and torn. I reached out for the best friend I ever had when the illusion faded. It was just a kid in a boy scout uniform, scared of the crazy man embracing him.

I retreated to an empty corner near the ship's store and tried to get my breathing under control. *Paul is DEAD. Dad is DEAD. I am not DEAD. Not DEAD yet.* As I tried to calm my racing heart, a woman, not much older than I was, introduced herself as the tour guide. She asked if I needed help. I took a breath and asked if Howard still worked here. She shook her head and apologized. In fact, she never heard of the old vet. Mom somehow found me and politely suggested I get some fresh air. We climbed to the flight deck and leaned against the railing, admiring the clear view of San Francisco. She seemed pleased and said how proud she was of me for coming back. I looked to her and nodded, trying my best not to stare at the dark figures circling the murky waters directly below. All this time, they had been waiting for me, and now I was here. They *needed* to eat.

* * *

Play It, Win It, Kill It

By J. M. White

1

Cal was the type of man who lived his life two ways: hard and fast. The hard was not equivalent to the hard in hard work either. And fast, well, the cigarettes and booze took care of that.

"It's so sad," his friends and family said. "He really could have made something out of himself. Now, look at him."

Ah, yes. Look at him now. He lived in an overpriced studio apartment in the outskirts of Boston with barely a penny to his name. He was thirty-five. He had no buddies. No girlfriend. No nothing.

Cal wasn't born into this life of loneliness. He had been raised by his parents, two upper-middle-class folks. They had stayed together, brought him to piano lessons, hell, they even fed him organic food. He went to college, majored in business, and got his dream job in real estate. He had been happy. It was not until he discovered his weakness that things took a turn for the worst.

***

Business trip.

That was what it was supposed to be. Cal and a few other guys from the agency had elected to attend a weekend conference in Connecticut. They planned to stay the night at the hotel connected to the Dancing River Casino, figuring they could catch a show and play some blackjack after the seminars. Cal had laughed at them. He'd never been to a casino before. He thought they were childish. After all, casinos were essentially extravagant Chuckie Cheeses designed to suck money out of pockets. Instead of flimsy, red tickets on the line, it was your hard-earned cash. Poker tables instead of skeet ball. Hot waitresses instead of costumed dancing mice. Oh, how foolish he had been.

The seminars droned on for hours. Cal had become restless, his friends worse. Afterward, they could not get through the glass doors of the Dancing River fast enough. They relished in the gold interior, the purple and blue lights, and the unmistakable clink of chips being stacked. His colleagues ran into that smoke-filled, windowless building the way kids sprinted into an amusement park. Cal had smiled, thinking that his friends had only proved his point. The scene had been significantly less exciting for him. The clouds of cigarette smoke constricted his throat, and the noise made him want to cover his ears. He soon found himself at the bar, seeking comfort in a glass of Jack Daniels.

"You fellas want to play some blackjack?" one of his coworkers asked.

"Sure. Let's start with blackjack, end with roulette," another stated.

"Or do we want to start with roulette, win some easy money, and use that for blackjack?" a third questioned.

Cal polished off the rest of his whiskey while listening to them talk nonsense logistics. He ordered another Jack and Coke from the pretty bartender. Cal would much rather spend his night talking to her than wasting his money on these dumb games that were probably rigged. After a few sips from his second drink, he suspected he might do just that.

"What do you want to do, Cal?" one of his friends asked.

What did he want to do? He wanted to order a few more cocktails until he worked up enough courage to talk to that babe of a bartender. If he was lucky, she'd pay him some attention. If he was luckier, she'd follow him up to his hotel suite.

"I don't know, man. I'm not much of a gambler," Cal responded.

"Dude," the more exuberant of his friends began, "we did not just drive two hours and sit in seminars all day for you to be a wet blanket tonight. Live a little."

The others laughed.

"Seriously, Cal," one added.

"I don't know," Cal responded, eyeing the cute bartender. An old woman to his left lit up a cigarette sending a fresh puff of carcinogenic smoke into his face. He suppressed a cough. His lungs craved fresh air. Maybe he'd take a walk around the place after all. He would come back to the bar, though. How could he possibly forget about the bartender? She looked younger than he was, maybe twenty-five. He could tell by her breasts. They were on the smaller side but firm. He liked the way they swelled out of her shirt when she bent down to retrieve a glass. Cal envisioned them in bed together, with her straddling him as she pulled her top off slowly, her breasts spilling into his face.

"I'll just play some slots, I guess," he muttered.

His friends hooted. "All right, grandma. Come find us if you want to play some big boy games."

Cal shrugged and meandered toward the machines. He seated himself on one of the uncomfortable stools and dug through his wallet to reveal a crisp, twenty-dollar bill.

"Here goes nothing," he mumbled as he slipped the bill into the slot.

The machine sprang to life. A mirage of electronic cadence drifted into his ears. Bright lights blasted him in the face. The game was self-explanatory: push the goddamn button, get five of a kind, win some money.

He watched as the symbols started to rotate, spinning so fast they transformed into a colorful blur before his eyes. Then, they slowed. Cal could make out some of the symbols as they passed. A neon blue seven. A bright red cherry. The word bar. His heart escalated the slower the spin became.

When the hell would it stop, he wondered. He wiped his sweaty palms down the front of his slacks. When had he started sweating?

Now, the symbols spun so slowly it was almost painful. Cal held his breath as they clicked into their final places: cherry, cherry, cherry, cherry... bar. “Dammit,” he grumbled. He’d been so close. Surely, if he played another, he’d win. Maybe not the jackpot, but a few bucks. His hand shot back to the “bet” button. Again, the machine greeted him with its burst of welcoming lights and music. He pressed the button to stop the spin.

Another close call.

He continued to push the button. It was mindless. Each time he was only one or two symbols away from winning big. After his tenth try, he thought about stopping, but something urged him to keep going.

One more, the voice whispered.

An old woman in a Hawaiian shirt won a few seats down from him. He watched with envy as she screamed, “Oh God! Jackpot! Jackpot!” The machine whirled and clamored before her as if in applause.

That’s when it developed.

The thing others talked about behind his back. The word that was only yelled in vicious arguments or whispered indiscreetly.

Addiction.

Cal continued to play slots for three hours straight that night. He never left that uncomfortable stool—not to refill his whiskey glass. Not when his friends told him they were returning to the hotel room. Not even when the cute bartender got off shift and walked past him. His prospects with her were long forgotten.

He only stopped when his eyes were red raw from staring at the machine. They hurt from focusing on the spinning wheel, pleading with it to land in a winning combination while wishing he had some sort of telekinetic power to control it. After, he wandered around the casino trying new games. He bounced from roulette to blackjack to Craps, then back to roulette. His pulse thrummed in his neck as he focused on the white ball whipping around the backdrop of red and black. He won five hundred dollars on one spin.

He continued placing bets until he was down to two hundred. It was a loss, but one he was sure he could earn back. The only reason he stopped at all was the casino closed at 3 AM on weekdays. He wandered back to his hotel room with his breath stinking of booze and the smell of cigarettes clinging to his clothes like an unfamiliar cologne.

2

Sometimes gambling had its perks. Even now, Cal looked back on those days fondly. But you needed to be smart. You had to make good decisions, which he did not. Sure, some of the money went to paying rent, buying groceries, and gas. But the rest was wasted on clichés like women, cocaine, and booze. He quit his job at the agency. The same friends who had brought him to the Dancing River eyed him with a mixture of envy and disdain.

Everything was okay until he fell. No, fell was too delicate of a word to describe what happened to him. He crashed, hitting rock bottom so hard it nearly snapped his neck. All the money he had won went to shit. His head had been consumed by addiction and clouded with cocaine and greed. He didn't invest. Hell, he didn't even set aside a few hundred dollars in a savings account. And after all the months of bounced checks, he finally lost it all at a green felt table.

The last hand of blackjack left him with nothing. He had bet everything and lost.

"Sorry, sir. If you have no chips, you're out," the dealer said. "Unless you want to buy back in, that is?"

Cal's hands balled into tight fists by his side. He wanted to slap the dealer upside the head and scream: Don't you get it asshole? I have nothing left, not a single penny to my name.

"Just give me a minute," Cal responded instead.

What had he done? How would he even eat tonight? Where would he live after this month was up? Maybe he could borrow money from his mother. Although, she probably wouldn't be too eager to help after all the other times he had "borrowed" money and never returned it. He shook his head, trying to clear it. He just needed a few minutes to think. If he could only—

"Sir, I'm sorry to ask you again, but please step away from the table if you're out. We have other guests waiting to play."

Play? How could he even use such a word? This wasn't Monopoly, this was blackjack and his goddamn livelihood. A sweat broke out across Cal's forehead. His heart slammed against his ribcage, threatening to escape. Curious eyes peered back at him from around the table. He turned to the man next to him. "Please, could you spare a few chips?"

"I'm sorry, kid," he responded. "Cut your losses now. It's easier that way."

Cal darted behind the man to interrupt a passing couple. "Please, spare a few chips. I'm—"

They didn't acknowledge him, not even with a polite nod of the head. They just kept walking. He whirled around and surveyed the crowd. So many people and not one could spare a chip?

Panic bubbled to the surface. He dashed toward an elderly woman and grabbed her by her pearls. "Ma'am, please. I... I... just need some chips. Anything," he said between massive gulps of air.

She did not take pity on him like he had hoped. Instead, she shrieked and pulled away. Her necklace snapped, a stream of white pearls exploding onto the floor.

"Security," someone yelled in the distance.

"What a psycho." Cal thought he heard someone else say, but it was difficult to hear over his pounding heart. Each beat that sounded in his ears almost resembled coins sliding into slots.

"Sir, you need to come with us."

Cal turned toward the voice. It was the manager flanked by two large men with "security" printed across their black shirts. "Please," he whispered. "I just need a few chips."

"I'm sorry, sir. You know the rules. Please just come with us now so we can avoid any more scenes." The manager's eyes bounced toward the old woman. Onlookers had gathered around her, helping by gathering tiny pearls in the palm of their hands.

Cal smiled at the manager before darting toward the bathroom. The security guards were on him in a matter of seconds. They grabbed him by the arms, his feet nearly lifting from the floor.

"Wait!" he screamed at the top of his lungs.

The guards ignored him.

"Please!" he yelled again. "Let me just..." He didn't bother finishing his sentence. Out of the corner of his eye, he saw something shiny.

A coin.

He wiggled out of the security guard's grips and slid for the discarded Coin like a baseball player into Homebase. He felt the metal's smooth surface in his hand just as the guard's forceful grips returned to his shoulders. A small smile played upon his lips. Now, he had something. He was not entirely broke.

The Coin felt big, maybe a quarter. Cal glanced down. The silver face did not depict George Washington as predicted. Instead, it had the grinning face of what could only be described as a demon. There was no writing on the Coin's surface or symbols depicting its worth. Cal's smile faded as a shiver passed down his spine. What exactly had he found?

3

Cal remembered that night like it was yesterday. He'd been removed by security and tossed to the cold pavement like a trash bag. He had limped to his car and locked himself inside. He rummaged through his Toyota's contents in search of a long-forgotten twenty-dollar bill, or maybe a few singles tucked away in the glove box. After a thorough search, he managed to scavenge a few coins. It was just enough to splurge on something from the McDonald's dollar menu or a lottery ticket. You can guess which one he chose.

It was utterly pointless, beyond an idiotic idea, but out he came with a single scratch ticket nonetheless. Cal dug in his pocket until his fingers brushed the smooth edge of the strange Coin. He used it to break through the grey film covering the lottery ticket while reminding himself that the Coin could be pawned for more cash later.

With each number's reveal, his heart pounded like he'd just run up five flights of stairs. With only a single number left, he cursed himself under his breath, mocking his own stupidity. He was just about to crumple the ticket and toss it to the sidewalk when it happened.

He won!

It wasn't much, only twenty bucks. But, hey, that was pretty good on a dollar scratchy. Cal cashed it in and bought another. He used the Coin, scratched the numbers, and won again. This time, fifty dollars. He cheered in the parking lot, pumping his fist into the air. Once again, he cashed in the ticket and bought another. After his third win, the convenience store clerk began to look at him funny. He started holding the tickets up to the light as if he thought Cal was cashing in fakes. Cal repeated the process of buying, scratching, and winning two more times before the clerk refused to sell him another ticket.

"It seems to be your night, my friend. But I'm afraid this will be the last ticket I can sell you," the clerk said.

Cal nodded. He could feel the heat of the Coin in his pants pocket. "I am feeling pretty lucky," he agreed. "This will be the last ticket. I swear it."

"Listen, I don't want any trouble, kid."

"What do you mean?"

"I don't know what you're doing, but I have never had anyone win five times in a row before. You're up to something, I just don't know what."

"I'm not up to anything. It's just for once in my life I think I've acquired some luck."

"Last one," the clerk reminded him as he handed Cal the ticket. "If you come back, I will call the police."

Cal frowned. He didn't like the man's suspicions, but it didn't bother him too much. Who said that money couldn't buy happiness, he thought, patting the Coin through his jeans pocket. It didn't even bother him that the Coin burnt his skin like hot coal. It didn't bother him one bit.

4

When Cal eventually returned to the casino, he didn't win. His new luck didn't work like that—there were rules. It all revolved around the Coin, the act of physically using it to scratch a ticket. Maybe he'd win if he bet the Coin in a poker game, but that was a risk he was not willing to take. Lottery tickets, on the other hand, were a sure win.

Consistent winnings had taught him a thing or two. Cal knew not to go to the same convenience store twice. Sometimes he'd drive up to an hour to cash in a ticket and buy another. Cal stopped buying scratch tickets after winning ten thousand dollars. The rational side of Cal told him it was a fluke, and if he didn't play his cards right (no pun intended), he'd end up penniless again. But the Coin didn't like that.

It wanted him to play.

On nights when he didn't, he had dreams. Horrible dreams where he was nailed to a green felt table in an empty casino. Then she would appear, a thin woman with slender legs that connected to an even leaner torso. Her head was adorned with long, sharp horns. Her fingernails were black and curled from length. She whispered into his ear over and over, her foul breath filling his nostrils, "Play it. Win it. Kill it."

When he was finally freed from these nightmares, Cal walked a few blocks to the bar. He ordered a whiskey, nursed it, and tried to push the nymph-woman from his mind, much like he was doing now.

He traced the circle of condensation his glass left behind on the wood bar top when a woman bumped his arm.

"Sorry about that," she said, her blue eyes sparkling beneath dark makeup.

"No worries," he replied. Even the slightest chance, no matter how minute, of returning home with this woman was enough for him to offer her a drink.

"Oh, I couldn't," she said. "I'm not staying long."

"I insist."

She smiled. "Well, if you insist..."

Just as Cal was about to flag down the bartender, someone tapped him on the shoulder. A man was holding his jacket. "Excuse me, but is this your jacket? It was on the ground."

"Thank you," Cal responded, taking his jacket from the man.

"It must have slipped off my chair."

"No problem," the man said, then dissipated into the crowd.

When Cal turned back, the woman was also gone. Dammit. He downed his drink and ordered another. When the bill arrived, he reached into his jacket pocket to find his wallet gone. It couldn't be. His money was in there, his license, but, more importantly, the Coin. Cal leaped off the bar chair and scanned the ground.

Nothing.

He ferreted around the inside of his jacket's pockets again, turning them inside out.

Oh no... oh no... oh no...

Cal thought of the woman. She had bumped into him so casually, or maybe not so casually. The man had tapped him on the shoulder right after. Was it only coincidence that they both disappeared? Cal didn't think so. He'd gotten played. And now those... those... con-artists had the one thing in the world that meant anything to him—the Coin.

5

He'd blown it again. Instead of admitting he had a problem and getting a real job, he had put all his hope into a stupid, worthless piece of metal. He had quite literally been living off luck. He'd thought the Coin had been unique, magical even. But there was no such thing as magic.

The five thousand he'd won was already dwindling. With the

month almost up, rent was due. He was, with no other eloquent way to say it, fucked. Cal downed another whiskey before dashing out the door. He stumbled back to his apartment and collapsed into his recliner. Before he knew it, he was smack dab in the middle of the nightmare he'd woken from only a few hours earlier.

He was in the casino, but this time he was not alone. The place was packed. He was seated at a blackjack table. It wasn't until he peered around that he realized nobody was moving, talking, or laughing. Instead, they were frozen in place like mannequins. Drinks paused on the way to lips. Cards clutched in hands. Their mouths turned up in wild grins depicting smiles much too wide to be physically possible.

Cal's heart thrashed in his chest. Something wasn't right. He placed trembling hands on the table before him, bracing himself to rise when she appeared. He collapsed back into the chair, fighting the urge to rub his eyes. She had not been there a second ago, he was sure of it.

"Going somewhere?" the nightmare woman asked.

Cal shook his head. This wasn't real, none of it. The stress combined with the whiskey had caused his unconscious to take a big shit in his head, producing this strange vision. A smile formed on his lips at the thought.

"Something funny?" she questioned.

"I know you from my other dreams," Cal responded. However, talking to his imaginary dream friend was so ridiculous that the idea had him on the edge of hysterical laughter. The cold seriousness in the nightmare woman's gaze caused any giggles to die in his throat. Her eyes glistened black, the whites concealed. Suddenly, she looked more demon than woman.

"I've known you much longer than that." She grinned, exposing a set of pointed teeth. "I know what you want, Cal. What you need."

He huffed. "Oh yeah, and what's that?"

"Money. Respect. Women." With the last word, she inched closer. So close, Cal thought she might sit on his lap. One of her pale hands jutted out, her black fingernails tapping the green felt table. The longer

Cal studied that hand, the more he was convinced it wasn't entirely human. "You want those things, don't you?"

Cal found himself nodding despite himself.

"I can give it to you," she whispered. "Would you like that?" Her long fingers caressed the side of his face. A shiver coursed through his body. It traveled from his head straight to the base of his penis. The beginning of an erection poked through his slacks. What was wrong with him. Of course, he wanted those things. He nodded again.

"Say it," she urged.

"Yes," he said.

She smiled and stepped back. Cal's erection faded. "You can find what you need in the glove box of your car."

"What?"

"Look in the glove box." She extended her hand, revealing two red dice in the center of her palm. "Go ahead, Cal. Roll them."

There was something about how she said it, the way the "r" hissed, that made him want to leap up and run screaming from the room.

"Who are you?" he asked, revolted by the fear he detected in his voice. Perhaps "What are you?" would have been the more appropriate question. She's a demon, the rational side of his brain warned. *Can't* you see that?

"If you see something you want, take it," the nightmare woman said. "Now, roll them."

Cal reached out, his hand hovering above hers. He reached for the dice cradled in the hand that he was now positive was not human. Lady Luck is a demon, he realized. Oh, God!

"Roll them. Roll them. Roll them," she growled.

Wake up, Cal. Wake up right this second, he shouted inside his head. He snatched the dice from her hand, threw them on the felt table, and did just that.

***

He snapped up from the recliner, his shirt soaked in thick sweat. The possibility that it was all just a nightmare did not stop him from sprinting to his car parked outside. He pulled open the glove box and began rummaging through the long-forgotten contents. He tossed aside maps, pens, and napkins collected from various restaurants in bulk. Some crazy part of him believed that he would actually find the Coin. Maybe he was mistaken. That girl at the bar hadn't stolen it. He'd simply gotten hammered and forgotten that he stored it in here for safekeeping. Maybe the nightmare woman was some horrific manifestation of his subconscious attempting to remind him of the Coin's location.

After emptying the glove compartment, he did not find the Coin like he had hoped. Instead, he discovered a knife. A decent-sized one too. A knife like this, a seven-inch, spring-loaded switchblade, was illegal in Massachusetts. Had he really bought that at one point? With no memory of doing so, it was difficult to imagine he'd made such a purchase. Then again, memories meant very little when talking about somebody who had spent the last five years of their life lost in a bottle and the white, powdery swirls of cocaine.

6

The following night, Cal loitered outside his neighborhood convenience store with his last twenty-dollar bill in his hand, watching his breath turn to steam. He was cold, miserable, hungry, and broke. The plan was to buy a couple packages of knock-off-brand ramen. He'd check out, saying "Thank you" to the store clerk instead of "Can I get four five-dollar tickets?" Then he'd go home, microwave his Styrofoam-tasting noodles and post up in front of the television. Tomorrow, he would figure out what to do. There was always tomorrow.

But the longer he stood there, the more impossible his plan seemed. He coveted each patron that emerged from the store with a bottle of water or some sort of cellophane-wrapped pastry. But what really caught his eye were the damn scratch tickets clutched in people's hands. His eyes stayed glued to them. It was amazing that even now, he itched to gamble.

Some people say addiction is a disease. At that moment, Cal believed that to be true. Some part of his brain must have come unhinged. Maybe blood supply had gotten cut off, or a flesh-eating virus chipped away at his rational mind. Of course, addiction was a disease. What else could explain his desire to choose the prospect of a win over food?

Cal shook his head. No, this time, he was not going to give in. This was his last chance to do the right thing. To his left, an old man hooted. He had been scratching tickets on the hood of his car, hoping for a win. And it appeared he got it.

Cal looked on with envy. For one crazy moment, he even suspected the old man of having his Coin. But that was ridiculous. Impossible.

He watched the old man hobble into the store to claim his prize. It must have been a substantial win because he returned with a white slip instead of cash. The nightmare woman's voice flooded his head. If you see something you want, take it.

Cal followed the old man. He trailed behind his old Chevrolet as he twisted through the dark, empty streets. Eventually, they stopped in front of a white ranch on a quiet side street. Cal observed the old man leave his car and waited until the lights switched on in the hallway, then the living room before exiting his vehicle. Take it, the voice reminded him.

Cal bounded up the front steps two at a time. He pressed the doorbell, and a smile formed on his lips.

"I'm comin'," The old man huffed in a gruff voice. "Hold your horses."

The man opened the door. "Yes?" he asked.

This was Cal's chance. Take it... take it... take it.

"I'm sorry to bother you," Cal said, "but you have something I need."

The man's already wrinkled brow furrowed. "What—"

Cal forced open the door, the switchblade he had discovered in the glovebox somehow already in his hand. The old man fell backward and stared up at him, eyes wide with horror. Cal thought of his mother probably at home in her chair watching the news. He thought of his buddies who had brought him to the casino for the first time. Then, he thought of the nightmare woman, and the last bit of his humanity died. He held the old man down as he cut into him. The man's screams had been maddening until he passed out. The body could only withstand so much. Cal barely even registered the warm splatter of blood across his face as he finished the job.

***

Cal ran to his car and locked himself inside. His heart was beating with raw excitement, pumping adrenaline instead of blood. He raised his trophy in the dim moonlight. The severed arm almost appeared to gleam.

Careful not to get any blood on the lottery ticket, Cal used the arm to scratch. When the numbers were revealed, he burst into laughter.

He had done it. He had rolled the dice and taken a chance. It was all worth it. After everything, Cal could finally say he had his luck back.

On that ticket, he won five bucks.

* * *

Satan's Town

By Bob Johnston

The newspaper headline summed up the situation rather well: "Last Minister leaves Satan's Town." George Smith finished his pint, rolled up his paper and left the bar. A few locals looked up as he walked past but no one said anything. No one ever spoke with him these days unless they absolutely had to. Even in the shops, transactions involved the minimum of communication.

He stepped out into a thick, sea fog and turned left for the hill leading to the bank. He walked cautiously. He doubted anyone from the pub would follow him. It was too warm and cozy there, but it was still early enough for children and teenagers to be about, and they had become noticeably more violent in recent months.

He stepped into the light from the ATM machine and quickly drew some money for the following day's shopping, before crossing from the bank to the lane opposite. Down a shallow slope stood the old Lowland Church where lights were burning through stained glass. He moved forward, placing his feet carefully on the uneven path, and made his way to a lit window.

A regular chanting came from within, but the window was a little too high for Smith to see in. A drainpipe ran down the side of the window, though, and Smith gripped it as tightly as he could and found a foothold on the wall. Feeling every day of his years, he hauled himself up and finally stood, hugging the drainpipe and looking in on the old church.

A group dressed in black robes sat in the pews listening to a similarly dressed figure who threw his hood back right by the altar just as Smith lost his footing on the slimy wall and fell to the ground. He landed on his feet, but his old knees gave way and he ended up in an untidy heap on his side.

He heard running feet and just had time to look up before he was hauled to his feet and held in a painful full nelson. The entire group appeared and stood about in silence. The man from the altar walked straight up to Smith and slapped him noisily, but not painfully, across the face.

"How dare you, Smith," he said.

Smith grimaced as his arms were pulled a little harder.

"I was curious as to how long it would take you after Reverend Palmer left."

The man signaled for Smith to be released.

"We bought the church fair and square, Smith. We can do what we like with it."

Smith stood rubbing his aching arms.

"I'm not saying you can't, Sinclair. Like I said, I was just curious."

Sinclair simply glared at him. He was furious, struggling to restrain himself. Finally, he spoke.

"OK, Smith. If you're so curious, come in. Watch!"

Smith shook his head and opened his mouth to speak, but Sinclair stepped forward.

"Oh, I insist, Smith."

Sinclair turned and walked back to the main entrance. The rest followed him, dragging Smith with them.

Inside, the ceremony began immediately as Smith sat impassively. He had seen it all before—the chanting, the unpleasant demands, the curses on enemies, the mumbo-jumbo. This ceremony was like every other pseudo-Satanist claptrap he had seen or read about. Claptrap finished, Sinclair stepped down from the altar platform and stood in front of Smith.

"Happy?" he asked.

Smith simply looked at him with utter distaste.

"Ecstatic, Sinclair."

Sinclair smiled coldly. He looked at one of the guards.

"Throw him out on the street. No need to be gentle. And Smith, we didn't bother the Christians when there were any in the town. Leave us alone."

Smith reached home a half hour later, lightly bruised, and noticed that the house had been attacked again. The kids had long ago given up trying to smash his windows, which were now strengthened glass covered with wire. Their trick now was balloons filled with paint. All the front downstairs windows were covered in yellow paint, and someone had crapped on his doormat. He sighed. At the moment, he was in too much pain to be troubled by cosmetic damage.

Pausing only to remove his shoes, he climbed the stairs and fell on top of the duvet. In a moment, he was asleep.

***

Smith woke the following morning and gave up any thought of shopping. It was just too much stress. He ate breakfast and settled down to do some reading. This involved a careful study of all national newspaper reports on events in Stanton. The earliest he had been able to find was from five years before when a witches' coven had purchased the disused Highland church. The outcry at the time had been enormous, and a ridiculous accusation of ritual satanic abuse by the witches against their own children had been made. It was finally thrown out of court, but not before a dozen children had been taken into care and the old church torched by town elements who remained at large.

Smith had lived in Stanton for more than thirty years. Over this period, he had made a special study of the rise of Satanism, coming to the comforting conclusion that most of it was sensationalist nonsense. Some of it was not, though, and the events of the last five years showed a developing trend.

For whatever reason, Stanton and a dozen other towns had come to the attention of dedicated Satanists, all protected by freedom of religious statutes. The churches had attempted a fight-back, but their ageing, half-interested congregations simply could not set coffee mornings against colorful ceremony and the (probably BS) promise of sexual orgies.

Smith had long studied the growth of these groups and had come to the conclusion that it was mostly harmless, if annoying, tripe. He opened a four-year-old newspaper at the announcements page and went to the ecclesiastical notices. The churches had gone mad at the advert, but again, the Satanists were protected by law. Along with the usual church announcements was one from the Church of the Beloved Satan: the "baptism" of four infants conceived during some Ceremony of the Expulsion. A ceremony never mentioned anywhere else previously.

Smith got up and opened the curtains. He had forgotten the paint attack and groaned at the sight of yellow splashes all over his windows. He lifted the phone and called in the vandalism to the police. Nothing would be done, but they would show up and take notes. Smith was a great believer in getting his money's worth from the police. They were all Satanists too, but they still went through the motions of being polite and doing their jobs properly.

Through all of this, Smith had attempted to keep some unity among the non-Satanists in the town, but in the end, the day-to-day pressure was too much, and most people had moved away. Of six thousand inhabitants, he reckoned only a few hundred in the town were not active members of the "church." And just to sweeten the deal, the Satanist always paid a fair price for the homes they were occupying.

The day moved along, and it was early evening before Smith found a reference, which really disturbed him. He lifted the phone and dialed Sally. A few minutes later, he painfully pulled on his coat and stepped out of the door, ignoring the foul abuse of a group of ten-year-olds at the bus stop.

Sally opened her door only after ensuring it was definitely him, and she swiftly shut it once he was in. She smiled, but he could see that she was exhausted. As an old lady, she tended to be on the receiving end of the threats and intimidation more than he was. But it was only a matter of time.

Smith spread out the newspaper and pointed to the column down one side. Sally put on her glasses and leaned forward to read.

"Spokesman for the Church of the Beloved Satan, Gordon Sinclair, said today that he is delighted that all the congregations in Stanton have united as one church. The arrival of a new high priest, Al Jackson from the United States, will be the final step in consolidating Stanton as a base for future expansion. Sinclair, speaking for Jackson, said that the church opens its arms to all and extends the blessings of Firsoudan and Bawisost to any who have an interest in its activities. This reporter feels compelled to say that events in Stanton (or is it now Satan's Town) must be viewed as a cause for concern. I had hoped that the death of organized religion would lead to a bright secular future rather than a degeneration back to witchcraft and superstition. God help us all."

Sally looked up.

"I wish those damned reporters would research their material better. It's this tying Satanism and witchcraft together that has caused so much confusion. If they'd spent more time looking for Satanists instead of bothering witches, we might not be in this state."

Smith folded up the newspaper.

"The only time people will see that there is a difference is when they've all joined Sinclair's damned church. This Jackson is the problem, though, not Sinclair. Sinclair is just an idiot. If Jackson knows about Firsoudan and Bawisost, then more trouble is heading this way than Stanton has ever seen."

Sally sat back and sighed wearily.

"Have you had any more trouble with your..." she pointed at his chest vaguely.

Smith shook his head.

"No. Just those flutters a couple of weeks ago. I'm fine."

Sally nodded.

"So, what are we to do?"

Sinclair shook his head.

"It's too late to mobilize the townsfolk to shun them. There's no point in getting the national press involved, the church is protected by law. I think the only option we have is to leave."

"And go where? Stanton is just the start. They'll spread out from here and from the other towns they've taken over. Eventually, there will be nowhere to go."

Smith nodded grimly.

"I know, but it'll take them some time, give us a breathing space."

They were silent for a time, but finally, Sally spoke.

"Is this Jackson character in the town?"

"I think so. Old Campbell saw a limo come in a few nights back. Look, I'll go back home and pack. Can you be ready to leave tonight?"

Sally looked about the small, tidy flat and finally nodded.

"Give me a couple of hours. Does the old car still work?"

"It should get us to Edinburgh."

He stood.

"I'll be back around midnight."

***

Deep fog had drifted in off the sea again, and Smith was glad of it. He could hear youngsters moving about, lots of them, but he managed to keep out of sight. The adults in the town stuck to their sullen silence, but it was only a matter of time before some teenagers took it on themselves to deal with the problem of the holdouts.

The house had been attacked again during his absence. Several footprints on the door showed that an attempt had been made to kick it in. He quickly closed the door behind him just as something heavy hit it on the outside and a torrent of abuse from several voices started up.

He climbed the stairs and pulled an already packed case from under his bed. He had been prepared for this for months. Taped to the case were the keys for the garage and for the car. He ripped the tape away and put the keys in his pocket. Then he went back down the stairs and stood at the peephole in the front door watching until he was sure the group of teenagers had moved on.

Some minutes later, he flicked off the main power switch in the house and quietly left. The garage was across the road and down a dark lane. He walked slowly and quietly. He could hear voices all 'round the area but, as he suspected, most of these youngsters were cowards who would not go into a darkened area where they might become the target.

He opened the garage door, got the car started, moved it out, and returned to close the door. He had practised this whenever he could, but even in the few minutes it took, he could hear voices approaching. He got into the car, locked the doors, and waited with the lights off. After a little while, a group appeared dimly through the fog and gloom. Their voices were raised, clearly to intimidate whomever was here.

Smith switched on the lights and drove straight at them. A couple dived over the hedge to one side, and a couple over the stone wall to the other. One or two stood their ground expecting him to stop, while the rest tried running in the direction they had come. Smith did not stop even after he had run three of them down. The car was not registered, so he was unlikely to be caught. He had just had enough of the harassment.

He considered parking inside the Lowland church grounds but decided against it. The church was the focus of the entire town's activities. An unknown car would stand out like a sore thumb.

Crossing the church car park seemed foolish, so he went round the block and approached the building by the same route he had taken the night before. At the rear of the church, he found a fire escape door which, not surprisingly, was unlocked. Before the Satanists had arrived, Stanton had been a town where doors were never locked. Now that it was all Satanist, the same was true.

The stairs creaked under him, but the voices he could hear in the church itself and downstairs did not stop. As he walked along the downstairs corridor, he could make out an American voice talking and pausing in a way which suggested he was on the phone. Smith peered into an office and saw Jackson facing away from the door, a mobile phone crushed between shoulder and ear. He leaned in a little to hear better just as a huge man appeared and threw him against the wall. Smith reached out as he fell, and his right wrist shattered in a blaze of agony. Jackson spun his chair around and saw what was happening.

"Sorry, Jack. Got to go. We've got an unexpected visitor. I'll call you back."

He disconnected the call and threw the phone onto the table.

"Well, well, well," said Jackson, "you must be George Smith. My colleague, Mr. Sinclair has told me all about you. And here you are, for what, I wonder? Why are you bothering me? What have I ever done to you?"

Smith cradled his clearly broken wrist and said nothing. Jackson shrugged.

"Fine. I am a peaceful man. I have no intention of repeating Mr. Sinclair's violence of last night, but plainly I cannot let you loose at the moment. I'm afraid you will have to sit through one of our... eh, services."

The guard pushed Smith out into the hall and followed him with Jackson at the rear. They climbed the stairs and entered the church. Sinclair was standing on the altar platform preparing himself. He raised his eyes skyward when he saw Smith.

"Good grief. You just cannot keep away, can you."

He saw Jackson come in at the rear and bowed slightly. Jackson nodded to him.

Smith was tied about the arms and chest after Jackson suggested that tying his wrists might be a little cruel. With a resigned sigh, Smith sat and Jackson sat beside him.

"Mr. Smith, I know that you object to our activities here, but at the end of the day, you cannot win. We are doing nothing illegal, and we are harming no one."

Smith remained glumly silent, but Jackson was not to be put off.

"I'm also sure that you think what we do is just mumbo jumbo, but fortunately for you, tonight is a special ceremony. Tonight, we will be invoking something powerful. Tonight, we will attempt to bring the exiled gods Firsoudan and Bawisost back to us."

Smith looked round.

"I know something about those things, and that really would be a mistake, Jackson."

Jackson smiled.

"Well I think I know better, and that is the course we are pursuing. I laid down all the preparatory incantations a couple of weeks ago, and there was a definite reaction to them. Tonight, we can finish and bring the exiles back."

Smith shrugged his shoulders against the tight ropes.

"Why Firsoudan and Bawisost? They're hardly top-of-the-line demons. Why not go for the big man himself?"

Jackson laughed.

"You might know a little about this, but you obviously don't believe any of it. Invoke the Lord Satan? I'd rather walk into a nuclear reactor. No, we revere Satan. We invoke the lesser beings. And as for Firsoudan and Bawisost, they are the demons of plenty. Our religion is one that values whatever existence we are in. If we are to live in this plane, then we should live well."

Smith laughed.

"I wish you luck, Jackson. Even if you succeed, though, I doubt you'll get one of Satan's minions to honor any commitment."

Jackson smiled and stood up.

"I think you'll be surprised tonight, Mr. Smith. I think you'll find Hell plays tough but straight."

Smith said no more but forced his hands round a little, so that he could gently hold his broken wrist.

***

As Jackson said, tonight was a special night, and the whole town was in on the act. The church building was packed, and cameras were broadcasting images to computers around the town. Smith had been placed on a small folding chair at the side of the altar platform.

The ceremony took its usual form. There was a long series of incantations that Smith knew were just crowd-pleasing gibberish. Then he heard Jackson begin the serious chants, chants he had heard before and that he knew were genuine. He felt his chest tighten under the ropes that held him. If Jackson had done those earlier chants properly, then this was going to be the real thing. But of course, he already knew that everything had been done perfectly. There was no mistaking what those terrible heart flutters had been weeks before.

The ceremony continued. Something was killed and blood poured over the altar. The room was hazy and spinning a little. Smith's chest felt like someone was sitting on it. This was bad now, worse than the first time. This was becoming pain instead of just pressure.

Jackson concluded the Latin portions of the incantations and moved onto the older Sumerian texts. As he began, Smith felt like his heart was about to explode, and suddenly, there was no more pain. He looked down at the ropes that fell away. He twisted the broken wrist a little and felt the bones quickly and smoothly knitting. As he stood, all the aches and pains of the old body he had inhabited for so long vanished.

Through all the decades of being Smith, there had always been a scrap of doubt about his true identity. When he had adopted this human form, he had taken it on so completely that there were many mornings when he had thought that he really was Smith, a rather sad, lonely man deluding himself that he was actually one of the ancient gods. As he walked toward the altar, there was no longer any doubt. He was, and always had been, Firsoudan, a demon of ancient Sumer, bringer of plenty at a price.

Jackson opened his eyes and looked up into the face of this hugely tall creature that was unmistakably Firsoudan and...

"Smith," he gasped.

Firsoudan placed a six-taloned hand on Jackson's shoulder and squeezed. Five razor sharp talons tore in through his shoulder blade and passed the thumb talon the other way through his rib cage.

"That is for my wrist, High Priest."

He turned and caught sight of Sinclair who was slinking away from the altar. His eyes flashed, and Sinclair hit the floor clutching at various parts of his anatomy that were now in flames.

"And that is for last night."

Firsoudan opened his hand and Jackson fell, grabbing at his ruined shoulder. The main doors of the church then blew open with a crash that shook the entire building. All eyes turned to Sally who had become Bawisost, an older demon than Firsoudan but one that offered much the same rewards. Firsoudan knew, though, that her price was always much higher than his own. She glided along the main aisle and joined him over the weeping form of Jackson.

"Is this the maggot who has caused us such trouble?" she asked.

Firsoudan nodded.

"The same. But still, we have a compact with humanity. He has called. We must answer."

He looked down at Jackson who had recovered himself a little.

"What do you want, High Priest?"

Jackson had prepared for this question long enough for it to slip from his lips and through his terror.

"Wealth, my Lord, my Lady. Great wealth for myself and for this church of our Lord Satan."

Firsoudan made a sweep with his hand and a huge mound of gold, silver, and jewels appeared surrounded by a great circle of dollar bills.

"As you wish. Now, for our payment."

He turned and faced the congregation and the cameras hanging from the balconies.

"It is customary to repay our gifts with service of some kind, but we choose to forego this custom on this occasion. The knowledge of what you have brought down on your miserable heads is payment enough. Bawisost and I have been in hiding in your world for centuries. We are outcasts from the world of demons, and that world has long been seeking us to exact severe punishment. Your invocation will have awoken every demon in this world to our presence, and they will shortly be here looking for us. Welcome to Hell people, and you brought it on yourselves. Enjoy your wealth while you can."

With a brief wavering of the atmosphere, they were gone, leaving a town less frightened than utterly confused. Three hours later, there was no further confusion as the first battalions of demons descended on the town in search of their renegade brother and sister. By daybreak, the demon world had thrown open its carefully guarded gates, and the entire hellish horde began the destruction of Stanton. As every attempt to locate Firsoudan and Bawisost came to nothing, the rage of the horde grew and grew. By the time they left a day later, the town was in ruins, and most of its inhabitants were dead.

***

Two days later, George and Sally wandered into the remains of the Lowland church. They were young now, and their happy smiles matched the sunny beauty of the day. They found Jackson and Sinclair nailed to opposite ends of the altar. Sinclair was dead, and it was clear from the state of his corpse that he had not died easily. His injuries were shocking. Sally shook her head and tutted.

"Messing with dangerous forces, young man."

George hauled Jackson's hands off the altar, tearing them past the large nail heads. He then lay Jackson in his arms and checked for signs of life.

"Yup. This one's alive, but I'd judge that he had some of the same treatment young Sinclair got."

Sally took Sinclair from the altar and laid him on the floor.

"Some of those demons do enjoy the nasty stuff. Never seen the attraction myself."

Jackson opened his eyes a little and after a moment recognised Smith. Smith poured some water down his throat and patted his cheek a little to make sure he was awake.

"Don't talk, Jackson. Listen. They'll likely not be back, but we have to get going. So long as we stay human, they can't find us, and the only way we stop being human is if some cretin like you invokes our names. Do you understand?"

Jackson nodded slightly, not noticing that Smith had reached into his pocket.

"So, High Priest, we have to make sure you do not invoke us again. It would be easy to kill you, but your pain is too satisfying to terminate so soon. But you will never speak our names again."

With a smooth sweep of his hand, he lifted a pair of pincers from his pocket and jammed them into Jackson's mouth. With a violent yank, he hauled Jackson's tongue out and leaned back as Sally cut it off with a single sweep of a serrated blade. Jackson's cries were choked off as blood flooded his throat.

***

George and Sally stepped out into the sunlight and stood on the remains of the church steps.

"So, you think that this increase in Satanism is a direct attempt to flush us out?" asked Sally.

George nodded.

"Why else would the demon world allow it? The likes of Jackson invoking demons at will. No, they value some contact with this world through wise humans, but this is different. They are taking the risk of being ensnared here in the hope that we will be invoked first."

"So, I suppose we just keep being careful."

George laughed.

"Well, why the hell not. We've been doing it for three thousand years."

They walked down the steps and made for the north road that would take them to the city eventually. And then somewhere small to settle down.

* * *

Everything as It Was

By Warren Benedetto

When I first walked into our crooked two-room house, Mama was standing at the sink, staring out the window at the barren fields outside.

The wind was blowing steadily, sending great big clouds of dust swirling through the air. It made a shushing sound against the glass, like someone was asking for quiet. There weren't any crops in our field, or the next field, or the next... or any, it seemed like, for as far as the eye could see. With nothing in its way, the wind just blew and blew forever, right through Oklahoma and into infinity, carrying all the dirt along with it.

I stood behind Mama and watched as she wiped a plate with a dishrag, round and round and round, real slow, like her mind was somewhere else. After a while, I opened my mouth to try and say something, but I couldn't get any words to come out. I guess I made some sort of noise though, because Mama turned around really quick. I must have spooked her. She dropped the dish onto the floor, where it shattered into a thousand pieces. Her face went sheet-white.

"Anabel," she whispered.

She put her hands over her mouth, then took a step closer to me. Her eyes got wet. She reached out and touched my cheek, then my hair. Her hand was shaking. It was like she was testing that I was real, that I wasn't some kind of ghost or apparition. Finally, she dropped to her knees and hugged me so hard I thought my ribs would break.

I put my head on her shoulder and let her hair tickle my nose. I could smell soap on her neck, and sweat in her hair. Smoke too. She wasn't supposed to have cigarettes—Papa said it made her smell like an ashtray—but I knew she kept a few rolled up in the bedrail, along the side of the mattress. She'd sneak a quick puff or two out on the back step sometimes when Papa wasn't around, blowing the smoke sideways into the wind, then snuffing the cigarette out on the side of the house and tucking the leftover stub into the seam of her apron.

Mama hugged me for what felt like forever. Finally, she pulled away and held me at arm's length, her hands still on my shoulders. She touched my cheek again.

"Glory be," she said. "My baby's home."

Mama ain't changed much since I last seen her, though I'd be lying if I said she didn't look older. I wasn't sure how long I'd been gone—six months? a year?—but her hair seemed grayer than I remembered. Her skin was looser around the eyes too, with dark circles, real puffy, like she'd been crying a lot. I suppose maybe she had been. Can hardly blame her. Times had been tough around here. Real tough.

Of course, the first thing she said when she saw me, after she caught her breath, was to tell me that I looked a fright, and to set about fussing with my hair. Appearances had always been so important to her. Even though we didn't have much, she always found a way to look nice. Hair done up in curls, lipstick on her lips, everything clean and tidy. She was a real looker, is how Papa put it. Used to be, at least. He'd say that second part with a wink, and Mama would snap him in the rear with her dish towel and say, "Dale! Stop teasing!" Then later I'd see her in the mirror, pulling at the skin around her mouth, trying to make the lines go away. They never did, for long.

After she swept up the pieces of the broken plate, Mama took my hand and walked me into the bedroom.

"I made a new dress for you," she said. "For when you came home." She opened the bedroom closet and rummaged around inside. "Papa said I was wasting my time, that you weren't ever coming back, but I told him, I said, 'My time's my business, and yes, she sure as heck is.' He wasn't too happy with that." She laughed. The sound was sharp and loud in the tiny, low-roofed room. "You know how he feels about sassing back."

Did I ever. If there was one thing Papa hated, it was sass. There wasn't any place for a girl to be talking back to her father. Or her husband. Or any man, really. Not unless she wanted a handprint on her hide. I learned that lesson the hard way. Only had to be taught once though. Papa made sure of that.

"I prayed on it though," Mama continued. "I prayed on it really hard." She pointed behind her at a small table by the bed where she had set up a photo of me, along with some melted-down candles, a handmade cross, and a small jar full of dirt. "I prayed that you'd come home, and the crops would come back, and everything would go back to how it used to be. And now, glory be, here you are."

I walked over and picked up the photo. It was a picture of me and Charlie Henderson from next door, taken by Papa at the Church of God Easter Festival a few years back, before he had to sell off his camera to pay for groceries. We were five, maybe six years old, both clutching these huge jackrabbits and looking just happy as could be. A big banner sagged over our heads, with the words "HE IS RISEN" painted on them in bright red letters.

I remembered that day so clearly. The sky was blue. The wind was still. There wasn't any dust. We weren't sick yet.

It was a good day. Maybe the best.

Maybe the last.

***

Pretty soon after that day, the dust storms started. "Black blizzards" was what people called them. They'd come across the sky like a towering black ocean wave, as far and high as the eye could see, just waiting to crash over us and wash us clear off the Earth. Except, instead of water, these waves were made of dirt. When they hit, the dust was so thick that we could hardly breathe. We couldn't even step outside without a wet towel over our faces, lest we take in too much dust in our lungs.

Mama said the storms were a test, that God was testing our faith. But Papa saw it differently. He saw it like God had abandoned us. All of us, all at once. We were forgotten by God, forgotten by the government, forgotten by everyone.

"A man has to make his own way now," was how he put it. "We're on our own."

I remember Charlie's dad, Mr. Henderson, answered "Amen" to that. That was a church word, which I thought was a funny thing to say to someone doubting God. But maybe that was the point.

Before long, people started getting sick, coughing, spitting up black phlegm. Dust-sick, they called it. Babies and old people had it the worst. It got the Miller twins down the road first, one then the other, a few days later. Then it took old Mr. Kleffman, and also Mrs. Robinson from the grocery in town. Soon, even strong men like Calvin White and Tom Frantz were laid up, their breathing sounding like rusty nails in a shaken tin can. Not everyone who got dust-sick died, but the ones who didn't coughed so bad, they wished they would've.

While we were hunkering down during one of the storms, I asked Papa why everything had gone so bad so quickly. He said we were in a Depression, and nobody could fix it, not even Mr. Roosevelt. That made me scared because, if the President couldn't fix it, who could?

I wasn't expecting an answer, but Mama gave one anyway.

"The Reverend," she said.

Papa snorted out a bitter laugh, then spit into a jar. "Some Reverend. Man ain't even got a church."

Papa was right. The Church of the Resurrection was nothing more than an old tent with a bunch of wooden benches and a raised-up stage in the front. The Reverend preached from behind an altar made of bushel baskets, with an old door laid across them. That was part of what Mama liked about him though. He didn't need a big building like the Church of God did.

"It means he's humble," she said. "He's regular, just like us."

"Humble ain't got nothing to do with it," Papa grumbled. Mama opened her mouth to object, but Papa kept going. "Just look at him. Regular folks ain't got suits like that. That's a city-made suit. Naw, he's a huckster, through and through. He just likes the attention. Wants to hear poor folks clap for him, to hoot and holler and shout 'Glory be!' at whatever nonsense he's spewing."

We had started going to see the Reverend around a year before. Things were about as bad as could be for us at the time. First, we lost our crop, then Grandma got dust-sick, then Mama lost her baby right when it was ready to be born.

For a while, Mama couldn't even bring herself to get out of bed. She'd just lie there with the crook of her arm over her eyes, a handkerchief clutched in her hand. Nothing Papa would say could get her up.

It was Mrs. Henderson who said the Reverend could help. She had lost a baby too, and started going to see him soon after. She said he was really something special. Said he claimed he could do miracles. That he was our salvation. That he alone could save us.

After a time, Mama wasn't getting any better, so Papa took us to the Reverend to see what all the fuss was about.

He was a big man, the biggest I'd ever seen. His face was sunbaked, with light hair that flew around his head like a crazy halo when the wind blew. He always wore a black suit with a long red tie, no matter the weather. He was a sour man. Humorless. I never once saw him laugh, or even crack a smile. He showed his teeth, sure, when it suited him. But there was no joy in his eyes when he did. They were flat and black, and his smile was mean. Cruel. The kind of smile you'd see a man make when a cripple fell on the steps and his groceries spilled out on the ground.

You'd think a man as big as he was would have a voice to match, but he didn't. His voice was thin and reedy. It seemed to come more from his nose than his mouth. The way he preached didn't sound like any preacher I'd ever heard either. The Mass we used to go to at the Church of God was quiet and reverent, with its hymns and homilies and silent prayers. The Reverend's Mass wasn't like that at all. In fact, he didn't even call it a Mass—he called it a Revival. It was loud and angry, with talk of demons and plagues and the Devil, of the End Times and the godforsaken ground. That's what he called it: godforsaken. Said Satan himself must've cursed the land for it to dry up like it did.

He'd get the congregation all fired up, to where they were shouting and cursing the land as if it was out to get them. I always thought, *How can land be bad? It's just land.* It didn't do anything except sit there and try to be left alone. It was people who were doing things to the land, not the other way around.

When I asked Papa about it, he said some people didn't want to blame themselves, so they took it out on the land instead. Maked them feel better to point their rage at something that couldn't fight back.

"Like the lamb?" I asked him.

"No," he said, looking troubled. "That's something different."

The lamb was still fresh on my mind, from the Sunday before. I didn't think I would ever forget the way it squealed and screamed, with four men holding it down so the Reverend could slit its throat.

I could see the whites of its eyes, staring at me, wide with terror, pleading. Papa tried to cover my face, but I pulled away so I could look.

I wanted to see. Until I did, that is.

Then I wished I hadn't.

I watched as the Reverend plunged his hands into the torrent of blood arcing from the lamb's throat, then raised his blood-gloved hands toward the sky. Blood snaked down his forearms and into the sleeves of his suit.

"Glory be!" he proclaimed.

The lamb's blood poured down the altar and soaked into the dusty ground. Mama and Mrs. Henderson and the others chanted and swayed. Spit flew from their lips and misted the air as they intoned "Glory be" over and over again in a rising swell of delirious rapture.

Papa was stone silent, his jaw set, his head slowly shaking side to side. He locked eyes with Mr. Henderson nearby for a moment.

Something unsaid passed between them.

Once the lamb was dead, we made a line and waited while the Reverend made the sign of the cross on each person's forehead with a finger dipped in blood. I felt sick.

"What's that have to do with God?" I asked Papa when we got home afterwards.

"Nothing," he said, taking a wet rag and gently dabbing at the mark on my forehead. "Nothing at all."

"Then why did the people let him do it?"

"'Cause they're scared, and when people are scared, they'll believe anything just to not be so scared anymore. To take things back to how they used to be."

"Are *we* scared?" I asked him.

Papa took a long time to answer. He looked over at Mama, who was on her knees in front of her small bedroom altar. Candlelight flickered on her face. Her hands were clasped tightly at her chin. Her lips moved in silent prayer. Finally, he nodded.

"Sometimes."

***

I took one last look at the photo of me and Charlie, then put it back on the table where I got it.

Mama was still digging through the closet looking for the new dress, mumbling "where the heck is the darned thing" and "if he threw it away..." Finally, she gave up searching the closet and went to look for it in the big trunk at the end of the bed instead.

Wax from the melted candles was pooled and dried on the table's scratched-up wood. I scraped at some of the wax with my thumb, then picked up the handmade cross and turned it over in my hands. It had been crafted by one of the ladies at the Church of the Resurrection.

The tips of the cross were stained a dark reddish-brown, dipped in the blood of the sacrificial lamb. I guess that was supposed to make it holier somehow. "Consecrated," was the word the Reverend used. Papa changed it to a different word though, under his breath.

"Desecrated," was what he called it.

The Reverend preached that the road to Resurrection was traveled on our knees. He said if we prayed hard enough, then God would bless the ground, and the crops would rise from the dirt, just like Jesus did. Our old life would be restored. Everything would be as it was.

As it was, again it all shall be, I thought, remembering the line from the prayer Mama made me say every night before bed. *The fallen shall rise. The lost shall be found. The taken shall be returned. Glory be to the God of the Grain, praise to the Prince of the Fields. Amen.*

That was why Mama took to praying all the time, why she had Papa build the little altar beside the bed. She brought in a jar of dirt from the field, along with the blood-stained cross and the candles, and made her own little place of worship. The picture of me and Charlie wasn't there at the time. She must've added that after I left.

Mama prayed at that altar every morning, noon, and night, asking God to bring back the crop, to bring back the rain, to restore what we lost. To give her a sign that everything would be okay.

Papa got pretty frustrated with the whole charade. He said Mama spent all her time praying into a jar of dirt, instead of actually doing something useful.

"Don't you see?" he told her. "Things ain't going back to how they used to be. Times have changed. We need to change too, or we're gonna get left behind."

But Mama didn't want to hear any of that. She didn't want to change. She wanted things to be the way they always were. Change was the Devil's work, that's what the Reverend said. God made the world just so. And it was meant to stay that way.

Eventually, Papa got to the point where he made a ruckus outside the tent one Sunday after the Revival, in front of the Reverend.

"I don't know, Pauline," he said to Mama. "All this praying don't seem to do no good, as far as I can see. On our knees every night and twice on Sundays, and for what? We still ain't got no rain. Ain't got no crops either. We got dirt though. Got plenty of that!" He bent down and picked up a handful of dirt, then threw it down. "Got a bumper crop of dirt. Dust too, hoo boy! You want dust? We got a special, two bushels for the price of one. We'll throw in a mud pie too, if you can spare a cup of water to mix it in. We ain't got none here, see?"

He said it like it was supposed to be funny, but it wasn't. Mama started to cry.

After he was done ranting, Papa got in his truck and sped away, leaving me and Mama behind. We had to hitch a ride home with Mrs. Henderson. She told Mama not to worry, that Mr. Henderson had lost his faith too. She patted Mama on the knee.

"We'll just have to pray twice as hard, to make up the difference."

***

"Here it is. Ta-da!"

Mama finally found the new dress, all the way at the bottom of the clothes trunk. She pulled it out with a flourish and held it up for me to see.

Like my other dress, it was made from the leftover flour sacks we got from the Relief Office. President Roosevelt knew that poor folks like us used the sacks to make clothes, so he did what he could to make them nice. Mama had found a sack with a bloom of pink flowers, like the kind we grew in our garden before it dried out. She turned it into a cute dress with short sleeves and a small waist, and a belt that she braided from different colored lengths of twine.

It was nothing fancy, but she sewed it up extra fine. It was pretty, I thought.

Mama shook the dress out with a sharp *snap* and laid it out on the bed. Dust went swirling up in the air in little spirals, then drifted down toward the floor. The way it caught the sunbeams streaming through the windows made me think of God. Like maybe He was still around.

Like we hadn't been abandoned after all.

"Hope it fits," Mama said. "Let's see."

She lifted my arms and pulled my old dress off, up and over my head. It was really dirty. Pretty torn up, too. She balled it up and threw it in the corner like it was trash. Then she slipped the new dress over my head and tied up the string in the back. She walked around me to the front, checking out the fit, tugging at the seams, brushing off the shoulders, picking off little pieces of thread and lint as she went.

While she primped and groomed me, I looked out the bedroom window at the Henderson's house next door. Their front door was wide open, with the screen door banging in the wind. *Mr. Henderson still ain't fixed that latch,* I thought to myself.

Charlie Henderson was my best friend. Always had been, since we were babies. We did everything together. Grew up together, went to school together, played stickball together, and—when the dust storms got so bad, they blocked out the sun for a week at a time—we got dust-sick together. Ended up right next to each other at little old Mercy Hospital up the road in Boise City.

And now, we were coming home together too.

I thought to myself, *I hope Charlie's parents are as happy to see him as Mama is to see me.*

Mama circled her fingers around my wrists, lifted my arms, and examined my hands. First one, then the other. "Oh my, your nails!" she exclaimed. She was right. They looked terrible. They were ragged and torn, with semi-circles of dirt caked underneath. "We've got to get these clean." She disappeared from the bedroom back into the kitchen. I could hear the water running as she soaked her dishrag and loaded it with washing powder.

While I waited for her to come back, I looked out the window again. I was surprised to see Mr. Henderson emerging out of their barn and heading toward the back door of their house. He was leaning into the wind, shielding his eyes against the sharp sting of the sand with one hand. In his other hand, he carried his rifle. He threw open the back door and disappeared inside.

Mama came back into the room, her dishrag dripping a trail of soap bubbles along the floor. She wiped the grime from my hands and cleaned my nails, then straightened up and took a step back. Her eyes got all teary.

"Glory be," she said. "Look at you. You look so pretty." Then she took me by the shoulders and turned me around to face the mirror, so I could see for myself.

I stared at my reflection in the dust-streaked glass. I didn't feel pretty.

The skin on my face was the color of dead leaves. It was dried and tight on my skull, and split in some places, exposing dull white bone underneath. There was a hole in my cheek where the teeth showed though, and a sunken black crater where one of my eyes used to be. I didn't have a nose. Half my lips were gone. I tried to say something, but my jaw wasn't working right. It just hung wide open, and a little bit sideways. That's how I could see that I didn't have a tongue.

As I stared at my ruined face, I could hear screams coming from the direction of the Hendersons' house, followed by gunshots. I started to get worried. *That ain't good,* I thought. *I hope Charlie's all right.*

I watched in the mirror as Mama took her wood-handled hairbrush and tried to brush through the mats in my hair. She was doing her best, but the bristles kept getting stuck. After a few tries, she gave up and put the brush down on the dresser. It had big clumps of hair in it, with ragged strips of rotten skin still attached. Undeterred, she gathered up what hair I had left on my head and started weaving it into a braid instead.

Suddenly, the floor shook under my bare feet. Heavy footsteps thudded across the front porch of our house, followed by the familiar squeak of the front door opening. A few more footsteps, inside the house now, then Papa threw open the bedroom door. He stopped dead in his tracks. His face went as gray as the Boise City Post.

Mr. Henderson entered behind him, still carrying his rifle. Red-black flecks of blood were peppered across his cheeks and neck and were splattered down the front of his white undershirt. His expression was grim.

Mama primped up the dress around my shoulders, then turned me around to face my father.

"Look who's home," she said. She smiled. Tears streamed down her face, cutting tracks through the dust on her cheeks.

Papa's breathing tapered down to nothing. He was silent. He closed his eyes and pressed the back of his hand to his lips.

Mr. Henderson chambered a round in the rifle.

With his eyes still closed, Papa reached out toward Charlie's father. Mr. Henderson handed him the rifle.

"Go," Papa said. His voice was choked, barely a whisper. Mr. Henderson made the sign of the cross, then backed out of the room, closing the door behind him.

Papa gripped the rifle in his hands, his finger rigid against the trigger guard. He swallowed hard.

"Anabel," Mama said quietly. "Say hello to your father." With a firm hand in the middle of my back, she guided me closer to him.

Papa opened his eyes. His face was pained.

I looked down at the floor, ashamed of my horrid appearance. I didn't want him to see me like this. I couldn't bear to have him looking at me. I wanted to crawl away, back into the dirt where I came from.

Papa reached down and nudged my chin up with the side of one curled finger. He took a moment to look at my face. Then he leaned the rifle in the corner by the door frame and dropped to one knee. He extended his arms and enfolded me in a warm hug. I hugged him back. The stubble from his cheek was rough against my skin.

I heard Mama exhale a shuddery sigh. She knelt down and embraced me from behind. We held each other like that for a while, nobody saying anything.

Finally, Mama lifted her head and looked over to the small table where my picture was. She drew in a breath, then touched Papa's arm.

"Dale," she said. She flicked her eyes toward the table.

Papa looked over. A sob hitched in his chest. In the small jar next to my photo, a bright green shoot of leaves was poking through the dirt. It wasn't like any normal shoot I had ever seen—it was twisted like a corkscrew, with a sharp tip at the end. But it was there. It was alive.

"Everything as it was," Mama said.

Papa placed a soft kiss on my forehead, then kissed Mama on the lips.

"Glory be."

* * *

Summer Camp

By Ron Ripley

Someone told Jimmy Hsu's parents that summer camp was a good idea, and they believed it.

Jimmy suspected it was Father Michael at St. Patrick's Church. His suspicion increased when it had turned out the summer camp he was going to attend was in Hudson, New Hampshire, at the Presentation of Mary Academy.

Jimmy didn't argue with his parents when they had told him about the camp. He didn't pretend to like the idea either. His mother noticed that he wasn't pleased.

Jimmy's father, apparently ignorant of his son's discomfort around others and with the great outdoors, left the room. His mother remained behind.

"This doesn't please you," she stated in Cantonese.

"It does not," Jimmy agreed.

"Why?"

He forced himself to think before answering. It was difficult, and it was something he and the special education teacher had worked on quite a bit. "Because I don't want to be outside."

She raised an eyebrow, waiting.

"And other children don't understand me. It will be a long week. I will have no place to be alone."

His mother nodded. "This will not be a bad thing."

Jimmy didn't respond.

"Do you want us to send you to Hong Kong for the summer?" his mother asked.

Jimmy shook his head. He knew there were relatives there who would be happy to see him and to help him stay abreast of customs, but it was too different. He struggled enough when it came to navigating the town of Anger. Jimmy couldn't imagine how difficult it would be in a city the size of Hong Kong.

"Well, this is the next best thing," his mother said, switching to English. "You need to go out more, Jimmy, not less. Last summer you spent far too much time indoors. I will not have it again."

Jimmy suspected his parents wanted what they euphemistically referred to as "grown-up time." Why they didn't state their desire for carnal relations outright, he couldn't understand. He filed the thought away. *Maybe there will be someone I can ask at camp.*

Aloud, he asked, "When do I have to leave?"

"Monday," his mother answered.

He blinked, surprised. "Tomorrow?"

She nodded.

He tilted his head to one side. "Why so soon?"

"We didn't want you to have too much time to think about it. I will help you pack tonight, then your father and I will drive you to the camp in the morning."

Jimmy accepted the statement, got to his feet, and left the room. It was nearly time for him to go to bed, and since he had no choice in the matter of his trip, there was no further need to discuss it.

The morning came far sooner than he wanted it to.

By seven, he had eaten his breakfast and was dressed, standing by the door as his parents spoke with each other in the kitchen. Their voices were low, and the words were difficult to understand. They were speaking Mandarin rather than Cantonese, and his knowledge of the language was not strong enough for him to pick out more than one or two words.

Finally, they finished their conversation, and in a short time, they were all in the car. His bag was on the backseat beside him, and in his hands, he held a new book his father had purchased for him on Friday. It was a large, old volume on fairytales and folklore in New England.

His parents kept track of his browsing history on the computer, and since he never bothered to use any sort of incognito program, they knew how much folklore he researched. They thought he read the information for pleasure.

What would they think, he wondered, looking out the window, *if I told them I knew all the information was true? At least most of it? What of the creatures in the woods, and the ghosts in the cemeteries and the houses?*

So many things are true, and almost no one believes them. Jimmy watched the scenery for a short time, then thought, *The librarian, Mr. Tate. I think he believes it. He is a man who looks as though he knows more than people think. I will have to ask him when I come back from camp.*

The idea of camp brought a sour taste to his mouth, and he must have made an expression because his mother cleared her throat. Glancing up, Jimmy saw she was watching him in the mirror of her sun visor.

"Are you well, Jimmy?" she asked.

Jimmy nodded. There was no need to lie and say he was not. He was scheduled to be at camp, and unless he suddenly developed a fever, that was where he was going to be.

Jimmy leaned back against his seat and picked up the book. He flipped it open to a chapter on sprites, and above the first line was a drawing of several small, winged humanoid figures tormenting a little girl. They were pulling on her hair, and her lips, the expression on her face one of terror and dismay.

Curious, Jimmy settled in and began to read.

By the time he finished the chapter, they were in Hudson and pulling into the driveway of the Presentation of Mary Academy. They passed through a large iron arch supported by a pair of massive brick pillars. The driveway stretched on for almost a quarter mile, the end of which was dominated by a tall and wide building of brick and marble.

Along the way, there were handwritten signs on stakes driven into the grass on either side of the drive. They welcomed families and campers to the school, and they promised fun and excitement.

Jimmy didn't want either one of them.

He wanted to be home, with his books or wandering Anger looking for the dark creatures he knew to be hiding in the town.

Or the library, Jimmy thought as his father guided the car around the building toward a large parking lot. As his father pulled into a parking space, Jimmy reluctantly unbuckled his seatbelt. Taking his bag, Jimmy opened the door as his parents opened theirs, and climbed out of the car.

He stood beside his mother while his father went in search of a camp counselor, returning a few minutes later with a smiling young woman. Her face was tanned, her blonde hair pulled back into a ponytail, and around her neck was a golden chain with the name Traci, written in script. On the bright blue T-shirt that she wore, there was a name tag, one that also read Traci.

The "i" was dotted with a heart.

With a sinking feeling in his stomach, Jimmy realized she was an older version of the girls he went to school with.

There would be no assistance from her.

Despite her being only a few inches taller than he was, Traci made a production of looking down at Jimmy.

"So!" she exclaimed. "You're Jimmy Hsu!"

"I am. You are Traci."

She blinked several times as if taken aback by his almost mechanical tone. Her eyes flickered to his father, then back to Jimmy. "Yes, yes, I am. I'm Traci. I'm a camp counselor here, and just like you, I used to come to the camp! I just graduated from PMA this past year."

"I am in middle school," Jimmy offered, attempting to be polite for the sake of his parents.

"Well, Jimmy," Traci beamed, her teeth large and white and even. "What do you like to do outside?"

"Nothing," Jimmy answered.

"Oh, you must be kidding! A big boy like you not doing anything outside?" She gave him a smile, which he was certain she reserved for toddlers and imbeciles. "Come on, you can tell Miss Traci. What do you like to do outside?"

Jimmy stared at her. "Nothing."

"He likes to walk," his mother offered from behind him.

"Hiking is my favorite," Traci confided.

Jimmy shook his head. "I do not hike. I walk. I walk on the street and on sidewalks. They are safe. The woods are dangerous."

Traci blushed, and he saw her make a small motion with her left hand. Off to the left, a young man started moving toward them.

"Okay," Traci tried to smile, but it was weaker than before. "I'm going to need to speak with your parents for a few minutes, Jimmy. I'm going to have Paul take you to your cabin, so you can meet your cabinmates for the week."

Paul, as Jimmy saw, was a male version of Traci. He was taller, but he was as tanned and with blond hair. The hair was long and combed back in a wave from his forehead while the sides were shaved. It was a style Jimmy had seen on some of his classmates.

"Hey!" Paul grinned, his teeth as large, even, and as white as Traci's. "How are you, big man! My name's Paul."

He extended his hand, and Jimmy looked at it.

"Jimmy doesn't touch other people," his mother explained, her tone cool. Jimmy recognized the tone; it was one she used with people she felt were being deliberately ignorant.

Paul dropped his hand, a surprised expression appearing then disappearing from his face.

"This is Jimmy Hsu," Traci stated. "Do you remember?"

Paul blinked and looked as though he was about to say he didn't, then understanding and recollection dawned in his blue eyes. "Right! Right! Man, I am so sorry! It's been a busy day. Plus, this weekend, my apologies, Mr. and Mrs. Hsu." Paul looked back at Jimmy and smiled. "And I apologize to you too, Jimmy. Anyway, why don't you follow me and I'll take you to your cabin."

Jimmy nodded and slung his pack over his shoulder. His parents smiled at him, and he forced himself to smile in return. Without a word, he looked at Paul.

"Oh, okay then," the young man stated. "Right. Here we go."

Paul turned away, and Jimmy followed.

"First time at an overnight camp, Jimmy?" Paul asked.

"Yes."

Paul waited to see if Jimmy would say anymore, and when he didn't, Paul cleared his throat.

"Um, do you like the outdoors?"

"No."

"What do you like?"

"Reading," Jimmy answered.

They lapsed into silence, and while Jimmy saw that Paul was uncomfortable, he was not. He preferred silence. The idea that he would have to share sleeping space with strangers was unsettling, and he wasn't certain how he would deal with it. When he was younger, he had suffered from a tendency to scream and lash out when the pressure became too much. He hoped he would not revert to that behavior.

Paul led him along a wide dirt path lined with large stones that had recently been painted white. A few other campers and counselors passed by, and Paul greeted almost all by name.

In a short time, they came to a row of cabins. Jimmy saw there were ten of them, five on each side. As they passed them, he caught a glimpse of an outhouse behind each one. He also noted the names on each of the cabins. Muskrats, Bears, Beavers, Fisher Cats, and various other mammals.

Paul eventually came to a stop in front of the last cabin on the right. The name over the door was Coyotes. Paul pulled the screen door open and motioned for Jimmy to step inside.

Jimmy did so, moving over to the left and looking around the interior.

There were two sets of bunk beds and one folding cot near the door. Beneath the cot was a pair of large shoes and a locked box. On the two lower bunks, there were duffle bags.

"This is our cabin," Paul stated, his voice pleased. "We're the Coyotes. Our sister cabin is the Wolves. We split everything between boys and girls. In here, we'll have four boys. When we compete in activities and contests, we'll be paired up with the Wolves. We eat together and do various stuff around the camp together. It's a lot of fun. Traci is the counselor for the Wolves. Which bunk do you want, Jimmy?"

"The right one, please," Jimmy answered.

Paul nodded. "Toss your pack up there then. Do you want to see the rest of the camp?"

"No." Jimmy placed his pack up on the bunk and began to climb the rungs to his bed.

Paul cleared his throat. "Well, um, I guess I phrased that wrong. See, most kids do want to see it, so, you know."

Jimmy climbed down and looked at the young man.

"By asking them if they want to see it, and knowing they do, you are giving them a choice when they really have no choice," Jimmy stated. "I have no choice. You will show me the camp whether I want to see the camp or not."

Paul blushed and nodded. Then, he forced a smile and offered, "How about this, I'll assume you don't want to do anything, and if you have an actual choice, I'll give it to you. If you don't, I won't pretend that you do."

"That sounds like a fair arrangement." Jimmy peered up at him. "Will I have time to read?"

"Yes," Paul nodded after a moment. "In fact, I will do my best to ensure you have some reading time every day. Sound good?"

Jimmy nodded.

"I'd say shake on it, but you don't shake," Paul chuckled. "Come on, Jimmy Hsu, let me show you the camp."

Jimmy and Paul walked out of the cabin, and Jimmy dutifully followed along. Paul pointed out various parts of the camp to him, but he did so in a normal tone, and not the feigned joyful voice that he and Traci used when Jimmy had first arrived.

As they walked, Jimmy saw the chow hall, which was a large tent set up a short distance away. There were also showers, an archery range, a painting section, and an open kiln for pottery. A path branched off, and they followed it to a large lake. Several piers extended into the water, and there were dozens of canoes tied up. Paul's voice took on a happier note when he pointed out the lake and the canoes, and Jimmy suspected the young man enjoyed being on the water.

"Do you fish?" Paul asked. "Wait, stupid question. Sorry."

Jimmy nodded, and Paul chuckled.

They walked out on one of the piers, and Jimmy looked into the depths of the water.

A chill surged through him, and Paul's words were lost as Jimmy focused on the sight below him.

A creature, vaguely human in shape, stared up at him. He suspected it was female, though he couldn't be positive. Fish swam over her, as did a turtle a moment later. She watched him, her eyes cold, her long, dark hair floating around her as shadows cast by the clouds above disrupted her shape. The creature in the water smiled at him, her teeth small and triangular, frightening in their strangeness.

"Jimmy?"

Paul's questioning tone caused Jimmy to look up and notice the look of concern on the young man's face. "Yes?"

"Are you okay?"

Jimmy peered down into the water. The female creature was missing. Jimmy turned his attention to Paul. "Yes."

"Um, okay, then," Paul smiled. "Let's head back to the cabin. Everyone will be meeting up there shortly."

Jimmy nodded and made certain to walk toward the center of the pier as they left. Paul noticed and chuckled.

"It's only a foot or so deep here," the young man informed him. "Not that bad. Can you swim?"

"Yes."

"Really?" Paul asked, surprised.

"Yes."

Paul waited, and when no further information was forthcoming, he chuckled and asked, "How did you learn to swim?"

"An instructor at the YMCA taught me. My father wanted me to learn."

"Okay, I'm going to go out on a limb here," Paul said as they started along the path. "Did you like it?"

"No."

"Can I ask why?"

"Yes," Jimmy answered.

When he didn't give an explanation, Paul laughed. "Okay, why didn't you like swimming?"

"The water is wet."

The young man laughed even harder, but Jimmy didn't see what was funny about the statement. Paul was still chuckling when they reached the cabin.

For the first time, Jimmy registered the noise level of the camp. He stopped in front of the cabin and did a quick calculation. There would be forty campers all the same age, he realized, and ten camp counselors.

There's probably a nurse, too, and one older adult, Jimmy rationalized. *There would have to be.*

His attention shifted to the school. *That is a religious school. There is a rectory off to the side. Religious people live there. They will serve as nurses and adults if needed.*

Someone shrieked in one of the nearby cabins, and others inside it laughed hysterically.

"Great," Paul muttered, "the pranks have already started, and it's not even dark."

The young man realized he had spoken aloud, and he hastily

smiled. “Well, come on, let’s get inside.

They entered the cabin, and Jimmy ignored the three boys his age sitting on the floor. Instead, he went to his bunk bed and climbed up to his bunk. The boys smiled at Paul.

“Hey guys,” Paul greeted, sitting down on his cot. “It’s good to see you back. Jimmy, those two boys with the brown hair, those are the Tomlison twins, Brian and Gordon. The other with the black hair, that’s Quint Plummondon. Gentlemen, the young man up there, is Jimmy Hsu. He’s a lot like Chris Little, if you remember him.”

The expressions on their faces, and the way they nodded, told Jimmy that Chris Little had probably been autistic.

There was no malice on their faces.

Quint asked, “Do you talk at all?”

“Yes,” Jimmy answered.

“What do you like?” one of the twins asked.

“Books.”

“Books, Brian,” the twin who had spoken said, slapping his sibling. “See. Not everyone likes to watch television all the time.”

“Shut up,” Brian answered.

“Come on,” Paul laughed. “Knock it off. It’s almost time for lunch. Everyone hungry?”

The trio of boys cheered, and Jimmy nodded, aware that Paul was watching from the corner of his eye.

“Good,” the young man grinned, “I’m hungry too. Let’s get some food.”

Jimmy was hungry, and he did want to eat. What occupied his thoughts, more than hunger, was a desire to understand what he had seen in the lake.

As he climbed down from his bunk, he approached Paul, who looked at him with surprise.

“Oh, hey, Jimmy. Are you okay?” the young man asked.

Jimmy nodded. “I have a question.”

“Sure, what is it?”

"What is the folklore of the lake?"

A quizzical expression settled over Paul's face for a moment, and it was one of the twins, Gordon, who answered the question.

"There's supposed to be some sort of monster in it," Gordon offered. "One of those, every-ten-years sort of monster that comes up and eats a camper, or drowns a camper, or tries to. You know, basic horror movie stuff. Nothin' really original."

As the three boys tromped out of the cabin, Paul looked down at Jimmy. "What did you see in the lake?"

The young man's voice was soft, but his gaze intense, demanding.

Jimmy disliked lying, so he told him. By the time he finished his description, Paul was seated on the bunk, his face pale and his left eyelid twitching.

"You have seen her," Jimmy observed.

Paul let out a weak laugh. "Um, yeah. You could say that. I was in a canoe with three other campers, and Albert, our camp counselor. We were doing a long pull, rowing the canoe from this side of the lake to the other. Once there, we were going to eat lunch and row back. I think we were in the middle of the lake when the canoe went over, dumping the five of us. I was under the longest, and that was when I saw her."

Paul stopped, and Jimmy counted to sixty before he asked, "What happened?"

Paul's focus was on the floor, his voice a whisper as he spoke from memory. "Albert was deeper in the water, getting ready to swim up to the surface when she grabbed him by the right ankle. He tried to kick her free, but she pulled him down. She took him. They didn't find his body for two days. They said it looked like his leg had gotten caught on a log or something under the water." Paul looked to Jimmy. "It happens, you know. A tree will blow over in a storm and go in the water. Instead of floating or sinking, it'll take on enough water to sit below the surface."

"You did not tell anyone about this," Jimmy said.

Paul shook his head. "No. Of course, I didn't. I was seven. No one would have believed me."

Paul's shoulders slumped. "She's back. She'll be after someone."

"Yes."

"I don't know what to do," Paul whispered, and he sounded much younger.

"Eat," Jimmy replied.

Paul blinked, frowned, and asked, "What?"

"Eat," Jimmy repeated. "We have to eat. Without sustenance, we cannot move forward. If we cannot move forward, we cannot stop her."

"Um, okay," Paul stood. "I guess."

Jimmy led the way out of the cabin. He had memorized the small layout of the camp, and he had no issue going to the dining area. As they approached it, he trembled inwardly, the noise of the other children far louder than he was used to. In school, the lunch monitors had kept the students relatively quiet.

No one kept the campers quiet, least of all the counselors.

The camp counselors had their own table, and they were louder than the younger children.

Paul hesitated, glanced down at Jimmy, and asked, "How are we going to find out how to stop her?"

"I will read my book," Jimmy answered, ignoring the growling of his stomach. "I will see if there is anything in it about a creature such as she."

With that said, Jimmy turned away and went to the end of the line. He picked up a tray and waited, moving along when it was time to do so. Soon, he was sitting with his cabinmates and eating baked beans with hotdogs and apple slices on the side. He had a large glass of water, and he ate everything in silence as quickly as he could. The others smiled at him but did not try to engage him in conversation. They respected his silence, which surprised Jimmy. His classmates in Anger rarely gave him space to be silent.

In a few minutes, he was finished, and after placing his dirty dishes in the proper area, he hastened back to his cabin. Once inside, he scrambled up to his bunk, dug his book out of his pack, and opened it to the table of contents. The book, which had been printed in 1886, had a curious way of labeling not only the chapters but what each chapter dealt with. It was, Jimmy realized, extremely useful.

In chapter seven, titled *Water Creatures,* he found a subheading of *Dangerous Women of the Lakes.*

Flipping to it, Jimmy opened the chapter, skimmed it, and found exactly what he was looking for.

> *From conversations with elements of the Anglican clergy, this author is given to understand that with the arrival of so many Irish papists in the middle parts of this century, New England has been infected with various citizens of the faery realm. What is surprising to this author is how such a large number of water faeries have been brought from abroad.*
>
> *The most notorious of these, locally, is the fey woman of Hudson Lake. This is not Hudson, New York, but rather Hudson, New Hampshire. This small town shares a border with Nashua, which provides a tremendous amount of jobs for the uneducated classes at the local mills. Nashua and Hudson have rather small Irish enclaves, but these Irish–like their brethren in Boston, New York City, and Chicago–have brought their ill-tempered faery folk with them.*
>
> *The fey woman of Hudson Lake has a tendency to derive both pleasure and sustenance from the death of children, and more than one family has suffered the loss of a child over these past few decades. At this time, only one child is known to have survived an attack. Seamus O' Riordan, aged ten years, was wise enough to carry a good, sharp piece of iron with him when he went out on the lake to fish. According to Padraig O'*

Riordan, the boy's father, when the woman tried to drag Seamus under, the boy lashed out with the iron, cutting the woman and sending her back into the darkness of the lake.

This anecdote shows us once again that iron is one of the few elements which can drive off the fey.

Jimmy closed the book and returned it to his bag. He was climbing down from his bunk when Paul entered the cabin.

"Did you find anything out?" the young man asked.

Jimmy nodded as he reached the floor. In short sentences, he summarized what he had read, concluding with, "I need a piece of iron."

Paul frowned. "Like, steel?"

Jimmy shook his head. "It must be iron."

"Sure," Paul said after a moment. "Wait here. I think I know where to find some."

Jimmy watched as Paul left the cabin. The young man hurried down toward the school, and Jimmy remained in place, his hands clasped behind his back. He considered what he had read, and he wondered what he might find if he was able to read newspaper articles about Hudson.

Maybe I can speak with Mr. Tate, Jimmy thought. *He could help me locate some information. It would be interesting to learn how many children drowned in the lake. Perhaps in other lakes as well. I might be able to find out what other waterways are connected to Hudson Lake. I must assume there were deaths in those places, too, if they were connected. Does she have a circuit? How does the death of a child sustain her? Why not adults?*

Paul's return interrupted Jimmy's thoughts.

The young man appeared flushed and out of breath. From the pocket of his khaki shorts, Paul produced a slim piece of rust-pitted iron. It was sharpened into a crude knife, the blade curved, and the handle wrapped with black electrical tape.

"We have a place where we keep confiscated items," Paul told him. "I took this off a kid last year. Seems he was having trouble with some other kids, and he thought this was the best answer."

Paul held it out to Jimmy, who accepted it. The metal was warm in his hands as he turned it over. Finally, he nodded. "This will do."

"Now what?" Paul asked.

"We go to the lake."

"Wait? What? Now?"

Jimmy nodded. "It is daylight, she is eager, and she is hungry. I think she knows adults do not believe children. Or she merely does not care."

"And that's terrifying," Paul murmured.

Jimmy considered the statement, then nodded in agreement.

"I can't believe I'm asking this," Paul said, shaking his head, "but what do you want to do about her?"

"I want to go down to the pier I saw her at," Jimmy stated. "There, I will sit on the edge and look down, feigning interest, and excitement. I am hopeful she will see me and take me into the water."

"What?!" Paul's eyes were wide with disbelief.

"You will be with me," Jimmy continued, ignoring the young man's outburst. "You will be there to help me if I am under too long."

Fear crept over Paul's face. When he spoke a moment later, his words were rushed. "I don't think I can do that. Go under the water, not with her in it. I mean, I don't know. I didn't believe anymore, didn't think of her, or Albert. You know, I convinced myself that I hadn't seen her, at least until you said you did."

Jimmy considered the young man's statement, saw the terror in his blue eyes and nodded. "If you cannot do it, Paul, I will do it alone. She cannot kill any more children. It is an unacceptable situation. Thank you for the iron."

Paul stood frozen for a moment in the cabin, and then, as Jimmy slid the makeshift knife into his pocket, the young man shook his head. Jimmy saw the fear beaten back and replaced with cold determination.

"No, you won't go down alone. It's bad enough I got you a weapon. No. We're in this together."

Together, they left the cabin.

Other campers were on the trail, all headed back to their cabins, laughing and calling out to friends. Some smiled at Jimmy, and he remembered to smile back, although it was difficult. Social situations were awkward and painful for him.

Walking toward the lake, Jimmy was pleased to see fewer people on the path. Soon, they were alone, and in a short time, he was on the pier where he had seen the water woman. Paul glanced around, a single vein in his temple pulsing.

Jimmy was silent as he took off his sneakers and tucked the laces into them before he removed his socks, neatly rolling each and putting it in the appropriate sneaker. After, he pulled off his shirt, folded it, and set it atop the socks and sneakers.

"Paul," Jimmy said.

The young man looked at him.

"Do not pay attention to me now. Ignore me until I am in the water. Do you understand this?"

Paul nodded.

"Excellent." Jimmy sat down on the pier and put his hand into his pocket, took hold of the iron knife, and peered down into the water.

Seeing his reflection, Jimmy forced himself to mimic an expression of interest, one he had studied while watching television. He peered from left to right and back again, and then, from the corner of his eye, he saw her.

Jimmy continued to look away as she moved in from the right, creeping forward, her hair billowing out around her as she moved through the water with the sickening grace of a crab. He swung his feet lazily, keeping a steady rhythm, even as she reached out, then up.

Her hand left the water silently, her skin dull gray and glistening. There were webs between her fingers, and her nails were almost black. A heartbeat later, her hand slid around his thin ankle. Her touch was cold, strong, and brutal.

Jimmy braced himself, and he turned to face her.

She grinned beneath the water and pulled him in.

Jimmy's thoughts remained calm as he took a last breath of air before the water closed in over him. He ignored the chill of the lake and the way she pulled herself up along his body. Instead, he concentrated on sliding the knife out of his pocket. Her mouth was moving, and her eyes were cruel. He heard laughter as she pushed him down, and that laughter transformed into a shriek as he plunged the iron knife into her ribs.

Her hands let go of him as she convulsed on the iron, and it took all his strength to hold on. He gripped the handle with both hands, his lungs beginning to ache, to scream for oxygen.

Not yet, he thought and twisted the blade.

The water woman shuddered and went still.

Jimmy jerked the blade free and shoved her off him before he pushed himself up to the surface. He came up under the pier, striking his head against the underside. Stars exploded in his eyes, and he blindly made his way out and into the sunlight.

"Jimmy!" Paul exclaimed, and strong hands helped Jimmy up onto the pier.

Jimmy took several deep breaths as he handed the iron knife back to Paul.

"You're bleeding," the young man said, turning Jimmy around. "In a lot of places. They look like claw marks. Damn. Are you okay?"

Jimmy nodded, feeling the first stings of pain from the wounds. "I did not realize she had cut me."

"Where is she?" Paul asked, glancing at the water.

"Dead," Jimmy answered. "I suspect she would be difficult to find."

"Dead?"

Jimmy nodded, then winced. Pain blossomed through his body, and he trembled.

"We're going to have to lie and say you were attacked by some sort of animal," Paul stated. "It's the only thing people will believe."

"All right," Jimmy agreed.

"It's too bad," Paul sighed.

"What is?"

"You'll leave the camp now," Paul stated. "Parents always pull their kids out when they get hurt."

"Not mine," Jimmy informed him. "I want to stay. My mother will let me."

Paul shook his head, confused. "Why do you want to stay?"

"Because it was fun," Jimmy stated. "And my parents want their grown-up time."

Paul blinked, then let out a surprised laugh. He bent down, picked up Jimmy's belongings, and said, "Come on. Let's get you to the first-aid tent."

With the sun-warmed boards of the pier beneath his feet, Jimmy walked alongside the young man back toward the camp, pleased with how camp had started.

* * *

If you enjoyed the book, please leave a review. Your reviews inspire us to continue writing about the world of spooky and untold horrors!

Check out these best-selling books from our talented authors

Ron Ripley (Ghost Stories)

- Berkley Street Series Books 1 – 9
  www.scarestreet.com/berkleyfullseries
- Moving in Series Box Set Books 1 – 6
  www.scarestreet.com/movinginboxfull

A. I. Nasser (Supernatural Suspense)

- Slaughter Series Books 1 – 3 Bonus Edition
  www.scarestreet.com/slaughterseries

David Longhorn (Sci-Fi Horror)

- Nightmare Series: Books 1 – 3
  www.scarestreet.com/nightmarebox
- Nightmare Series: Books 4 – 6
  www.scarestreet.com/nightmare4-6

Sara Clancy (Supernatural Suspense)

- Banshee Series Books 1 – 6
  www.scarestreet.com/banshee1-6

For a complete list of our new releases and best-selling horror books, visit www.scarestreet.com/books

See you in the shadows,
Team Scare Street

Printed in Great Britain
by Amazon

48700675R00129